WAR OF HEARTS
Copyright ©2022 Susan Harris
All rights reserved.

ISBN: **978-1-63422-524-3** (paperback)
ISBN: **978-1-63422-518-2** (e-book)
Cover Design by: Gem Promotions
Typography by: Gem Promotions
Proofing by: Ashley Brilinski

WAR
OF HEARTS

◆────────────────────────────◆

SICARIUS SECURITY BOOK 4

SUSAN HARRIS

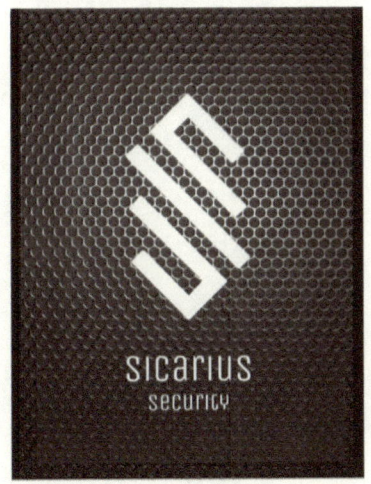

Aut inveniam viam aut faciam
"I shall either find a way or make one."
Dylan McGrath

Non est ad astra mollis e terris via
"There is no easy way from Earth to the stars."
Callista Rayne

CHAPTER ONE

Dylan

BY THE OLD GODS AND THE NEW, DYLAN WAS FUCKING starving.

He had not known hunger like this since the first time he was made into a vampire, where the bloodlust was all-consuming, that gnawing in his stomach like a sucker punch to his gut. Sweat soaked his skin, the tremors from trying to reign in the hunger racking his body as Dylan tried to ignore the succubus curled in the corner cradling her stomach.

"Dylan..." Scarlett said softly, his gaze snapping to hers as his lips curled into a snarl.

"No."

Scarlett huffed out an exhausted breath. Not that Dylan blamed her, he tended to have that affect on a lot of people but his sort of sister-in-law had been trying to get him to feed off her the last two weeks since Dante had been starving him, knowing just how much it would be like a knife in Dylan's chest if he hurt Scarlett.

Another blast of hunger drowned him and Dylan placed his hands on the side of his head to try and ride it out. Fucking Dante. Dylan should have known that the fucker could never die. Once Dante had revealed himself as Vindicta, Dylan kicked himself for not realizing sooner that it was their other sibling that was out for their blood.

It had been an immense shock to see Dante in the flesh, though his brother was not as he once was. That was pretty clear to Dylan from the moment he had woken up after being knocked out by his brother's pet Inferna.

"Don't you dare fucking touch her."

Vindicta had lashed out with his magic, sending Dylan flying back into the bars, hitting them hard enough for his spine to ache. Dylan watched his captor, felt the magic struggle for control and Dylan wondered how much of the power in Dante's veins was borrowed.

"You always were the defender of the weak." Vindicta snarled at him. "You always were the one who wanted to play the hero. It must kill you that the monster got the girl. That everyone around you has fallen prey to their lust and their love and you are still alone. If I still had a heart, it would be warmed now."

"You don't know fuck all about me." Dylan snarled right back at Vindicta as he pulled the hair back from his face and tried to see who his captor was underneath his cloak and hood.

Vindicta laughed at Dylan, Dylan's lips tipping into a snarl as Vindicta said, "But that is where you are wrong. I know all about you Dylan, about Malakai and Jasmine. I even know about the stray animal you all brought home."

Dylan sat up, Scarlett shuffling closer to him, but Dylan kept his eyes on Vindicta. Their captor took a step out of the shadows, then lowered his hood to reveal a ghost from his past that Dylan never thought he'd see ever again, and the surprise was evident on his face as Dylan shrank against the bars so hard they rattled.

Dante stood before him but his brother was not as he once was. Hidden under a glamour of magic were markings on his flesh that held stolen magics within his vampire body. It made his skin look even paler than normal for a vampire.

"What the hell is going on? You're dead." Dylan couldn't mask the utter shock in his voice and if the smirk that was threatening to curve Dante's lips was anything to go by, the son of a bitch was enjoying this slow torture.

"You should know by now, dear brother," Dante said, as Scarlett

sucked in a shaky breath. *"That sometimes, the dead do not stay that way."*

Dylan lunged toward the bars of the cage. "Let us out of here. You can't be fuckin serious."

Dante swiped a hand out and magic lashed Dylan's skin, sending his body backward, blood trickling from the slice on his cheek.

Dante glanced at his minion. "Callista, let's leave our guests to get comfortable before the fun starts. Make sure the succubus eats and drinks. Keep my brother hungry. Let's see how strong his willpower is."

Callista...that was her name.

Dante strode to the door, as Callista glanced at him, a blank expression on her face as she regarded him, the hellhounds gathering around the door to keep guard as Dylan growled and shouted. "Dante! Dante! Come back here!"

Dante had never been happy that his brothers and sister had power, when he had none. His entire existence as a human, then as a vampire, and now, as whatever in all hell he was, the jealously was still eating at him. But now, Dylan could almost taste the waves of stolen power flowing from Dante.

Scarlett shifted uncomfortably on the cage floor, causing the predator in Dylan to track her movement. The vein on her neck pulsed, the scent of her fear and worry making Dylan's fangs throb. A growl rumbled in Dylan's throat, causing Scarlett's blue eyes to clash with his and that pulse on her neck started to race. Dylan heard her heartbeat, quick and full of what he needed to sate his hunger.

Dylan only realized that he had gotten into a crouch when he heard another softer heartbeat that had him hissing and throwing himself at the bars in frustration.

"Dante! You bastard! Get your ass in here right now!"

Dylan knew that he was wasting his time calling Dante because since the night they had been ambushed and he and

Scarlett kidnapped, Dante had remained away from the cage. Food had been sent in for Scarlett to eat, and it had taken Dylan a few days to convince her that she needed to eat for the baby's sake. If Dante hadn't left them in a magical faraday cage that blocked his powers, he could have used them to persuade Scarlett, but Dante had been prepared for it.

His brother was enjoying torturing him and Dylan knew that if he didn't get blood in the next few days, then the bloodlust would overrule his control, and he wouldn't care that Scarlett was his family and pregnant; the hunger would be all that mattered.

Dylan knew that Scarlett had seen her mate Ezekiel Collins at his worst and she had loved him regardless. She had withstood the darkness in Zeke and embraced it. But that was different. Zeke was her lover, and father of her child. Dylan would never forgive himself if he hurt Scarlett.

It was a blessing, he supposed, that his empathic powers had been dampened because it was hard enough trying to deal with his own feelings, and if he had to try and process Scarlett's too, then he would be an even bigger mess than he was right now.

Dylan sank back down to the ground and hugged his knees to his chest, closing his eyes, trying again to contact Malakai.

Kai?

His brother Malakai Cavanagh could hear a person's thoughts and speak into their minds, sometimes, like with him and their sister Jasmine, over long distances. It always struck him as remarkable how Kai could remain so calm and collected when hundreds of peoples' thoughts raced through his mind, not ever showing anyone that he was in any way struggling. Kai had told Dylan once when he had asked, that it was much harder to handle an emotion than a thought.

Their sister, Jazz, had visions of the future. Himself and Malakai had protected that secret for many a decade to keep

Jazz safe and out of the clutches of Inferna who would want to use Jazz for their own gains.

He really hoped his sister had allowed herself to love her werewolf.

Dylan had known that both Roman Lowe, a werewolf who could not change into wolf form, and one of the best security staff on the Sicarius Security payroll, and his hard-headed but soft-hearted sister had feelings for each other since he was first in the same room as them. He didn't need his empathic powers to see the chemistry between them; you'd have to be blind not to see that they were inevitable.

Just like Malakai and his banshee bride, Keeva Cross. Just like Ezekiel and Scarlett.

His heart ached with a phantom pain and Dylan rubbed at the sudden jolt, knowing it was ridiculous to feel a pain in the organ that no longer beat. It reminded him of something Zeke had said, back when he had apologized for letting Dylan swallow Zeke's emotions, finding a way through his darkness to find love with Scarlett.

Zeke rested a hand on Dylan's shoulder. "First Malakai, now me ... Be careful, Dylan, because you might be next."

Dylan had let loose a surprised and horrified laugh, knowing that he would prefer to spend an eternity alone rather than wonder if he even had feelings for a partner, because it had been a long time since he had known his own feelings. "Not likely, mate, not fucking likely."

To be honest, sitting in this magic-blocking cage had been the first time in centuries that his thoughts and his feelings were his own. He knew that he was filled with a seething rage that belonged to him, and he had a longing to rip Dante's spine from his flesh and use it as a back scratcher.

He knew the immense hunger plucking at the unravelling strings of his control was all his, and while he fucking despised being imprisoned and powerless, it was a relief to just be Dylan and not crushed under the weight of everyone's emotions.

"Ouch."

Dylan felt sheepish for his thoughts, looking over to where Scarlett was rubbing her stomach.

"You okay?" He managed to grind out through gritted teeth, his fangs elongated in his mouth and giving him a slight lisp as he spoke.

Scarlett nodded, giving him a warm smile. "She's just active. Seems like she takes after her father's side and likes to be awake at night."

Dylan made the mistake of inhaling, the sweet scent that he knew was all Scarlett invading his senses and Dylan couldn't stop himself from imagining sinking his fangs into her creamy skin, piercing the flesh, and drinking his fill of her. He could almost taste her on his tongue as his throat burned.

Jerking back, Dylan smacked into the bars with a groan, shaking his head as he clenched his fists and punched the concrete floor, the skin on his knuckles breaking as his bone crunched and he cursed, knowing he didn't have enough blood in his system to heal it and now, because he had been reckless, the hunger would be even worse.

"Well, that was smart."

Dylan rolled his eyes at the succubus. "I never claimed to be smart, darling. Handsome, yes. Smart, never."

Scarlett snorted but she was smiling a little and that made Dylan feel a bit better. He loved Scarlett, he did. And for a while, during one of his really bad days, Dylan had worried that he had fallen for the succubus. But he had been relieved to figure out it was Zeke's emotions that were driving him. He would never admit it to anyone, though knowing Malakai, he had discerned the thought from his jumbled mind and simply said nothing, leaving Dylan to come to the realization himself that he wasn't *in* love with Scarlett.

Then there was his brother's blue-haired minion. Dylan

had felt her presence before in Dante's, their family bar, and being near to her had blocked out the emotions of others. He just felt nothing when she was nearby. His body had filled with anticipation every time she was close but he hadn't known who she was until the night he and Scarlett had been taken.

Dylan had heard her tell Scarlett to come with her and no one else would get hurt and her tone had been arctic, no emotion at all, and Dylan had been trying to figure out what kind of Inferna she was for the past two weeks. The Inferna never spoke to him directly when she brought in Scarlett's food, taking a bite of the meal to show Scarlett it was fine before she turned her steely gaze on him for a fleeting moment.

The way she looked at him, it ignited feelings in Dylan that he had long forgotten he possessed. Of course, when he took a partner to bed, he wanted to have sex with them, but it was more about scratching an itch, feeding a hunger. He was never a stay- the - day kinda lover, much preferring the frantic fucks in the storeroom at the club, men and women, hell even both at the same time.

His sister called him a sexual deviant, but Dylan spent a lot of time experimenting trying to figure out what he liked, because a lot of the time, what started out with him being attracted to someone, ending up with him drowning in his partners' emotions, their wants, their needs, and it left him feeling empty and hollow.

And of course, when he looked at Callista he wanted to know just how much it would take to thaw the coldness that seemed to seep from her entire being.

Footsteps sounded out in the hall and Dylan leapt into action, shielding Scarlett even though his hunger was almost enough to bring him to his knees. The heavy door opened and Dante strode in, Callista following after, a hellhound by her side.

Dante was dressed in black pants and a long-sleeved top, masking the symbols carved into his skin from view so Dylan couldn't decipher their origin. Callista was dressed in a similar outfit, but she had armour on her arms and legs. Her fingers twitched like she was used to carrying a weapon, but her gaze continued to watch him, without so much as blinking, the bright green of her eyes a contrast to the blue of her hair.

"Nice to see you haven't broken yet, brother."

"You could never beat me in a fair fight, Dante. Tell ya what, bro. Feed me and fight me. Let's see who would win then."

Dante laughed, shaking his head. "I've already won, Dylan. I have the succubus. All I need to do is wait the remainder of her pregnancy out. If you don't kill her first."

Knowing that eventually the hunger for blood would win out, Dylan couldn't be confident that he wouldn't kill Scarlett if he drank from her. The bloodlust wouldn't care if she was dying, only that it was being sated.

Dante tapped his chin like he was contemplating his next course of action, when Dylan knew the asshole had his plan all set out before he walked in the door. "I have a task for you."

"Like I'm gonna do anything you ask me to." Dylan felt Scarlett's fingers grip the back of his t-shirt.

"Then perhaps I'll have Callista cut the infant from its mother's womb and get rid of the leverage. I don't need the incubator. Callista?"

Dylan slid his gaze to Callista, who held up her hand and talons morphed from her fingernails, her eyes shifting shape as the wicked bird-like claws finally gave Dylan the answer as to what Callista was. Harpies were ancient creatures who rarely left their home in Greece. They were known for being emotionless beasts who cared for nothing but the kill.

How the hell had Dante acquired a goddamn harpy?

Callista closed her fist, the talons changing back to human hands and her eyes changed to appear more human-like. But it did nothing to hide the fact that Callista was a threat Dylan needed to nullify if it meant getting him and Scarlett out of here alive.

"I will end you, Dante. I swear it on the old gods and the new."

Something flashed in Dante's eyes that Dylan couldn't decode but then the other vampire laughed. "Your gods mean nothing to me, Dylan. I bow to no mere token gods. I am becoming a god."

"You're fucking crazy. Certifiably insane."

Dante glared at him, muttering under his breath, and then suddenly Dylan was coughing, blood sputtering from his mouth, spewing out onto the floor. Pain seared his body, and he trembled, falling to his hands and knees as he continued to vomited blood.

As suddenly as it started, the pain went. Dylan lifted his head and wiped his mouth with the back of his hand. "Temper, temper, brother. You always had a quick trigger. Oh, or was that what the women used to say? Sorry, blood loss is affecting my memory."

If looks could kill, then Dante would have murdered him many times over.

"Enough of this." Dante said, glancing from Scarlett to Dylan. "You will do all that I ask or I will cut the child from the womb and deliver Ezekiel his dead mate back to him."

Dylan got to his feet, leaning against the bars, without saying anything so that forced Dante to keep speaking, revealing a little bit more of his plan with every word.

"You will go back to Sicarius and retrieve for me the lost pages of the book of Lucifer. I had hoped to employ the banshee to do it, but Angus couldn't even manage that. I know Ezekiel has them, so don't even try denying it."

Dylan snorted. "The moment I step foot inside that building, everyone will know I'm there. How the hell am I supposed to get in, get the pages, and out again without being spotted?"

"That seems very much like a you problem. Besides, I find it hard to believe that the mind that created the AI that controls the entire building doesn't have a failsafe in place. You may like to pretend that you are hapless, Dylan. But I know it's as much a rouse as Jasmine's party girl front."

Dylan folded his arms across his chest. "I'm gonna need to feed before I can focus enough to devise a plan. It's not going to be easy, no matter if I designed the code or not."

Dante waved his hand. "Callista, give him your wrist."

There was a fleeting look of emotion that Dylan found very interesting for a creature who was supposed to be unfeeling, as Callista stared at Dante. "Sir?"

Red flashed in Dante's eyes and Callista flinched, gritting her teeth. "As you wish, sir."

So, the harpy was not as emotionless as he thought. Interesting. Perhaps he could work on her and see if his suspicions were true. Dante had shown him a chink in his armour and Dylan was only too happy to exploit it.

CHAPTER TWO

Callista

CALLISTA TRIED TO SCHOOL HER EXPRESSION AND REACTION TO Vindicta's order, yet, she could feel the vampire studying her, his blue-green eyes almost always on her even when Vindicta was speaking. And of course, as part of her recognisance, Callista had spent a lot of time watching the vampire. Her main focus had always been to watch the succubus and the obscurum, but it was the blond vampire who had snared her attention from the moment their paths had crossed.

She was not entirely sure what about this particular vampire made her curious. It was harder to pretend that her emotions were switched off. For centuries Callista had managed to hide the fact that she was not like those from her Nest of harpies. It was the very reason her mother had traded her to Vindicta all those centuries ago instead of killing her.

As a young harpy when she had fallen during training, tears had cascaded down her cheeks and continued to do so even as the elders in the Nest tried to beat the emotions from her. Her mother blamed it on her father, a beautiful human male who had snared Aella's attention, and his weak blood-line. Harpies might be emotionless but they still needed to reproduce, and they liked to rut.

Callista had tried to ignore her human side, forcing herself to train and push down her emotions for the sake of remaining with her mother, with her kin, and yet her mother had cast her from the Nest the moment a stranger had offered her coin.

It had been centuries since Callista had seen Aella, not returning to Greece since she had been bound to serve Vindicta. There had been times over the years when it had not been so bad, but in the last couple of years, Vindicta's moods had become more erratic and the moments of clarity less and less.

Even now as he offered Callista to the vampire like she were nothing more than a meal, Callista had to swallow down the white-hot rage that heated her veins. The strangely appealing vampire arched a brow as if in challenge, the corners of his full lips quirking.

Rolling up her sleeve, Callista couldn't help but watch as the vampire's eyes tracked her movements, and she willed herself to remain stoic. She had never been bitten by a vampire before, and it was not something she wanted to experience, though she was glad it was this vampire and not the one who held her reins.

She willed her talons to stay sheathed, easing her hand through the bars of the cage, her eyes trained on the vampire who licked his lips. Callista was cautious that Vindicta was watching the exchange intently as if he expected Callista to disobey his orders.

But he knew by now that she would not…she could not.

When the vampire made no attempt to come forward, Callista lifted her gaze to Vindicta, then back to the vampire.

"I thought you were starving, Dylan."

The vampire, Dylan, snorted. "I won't drink from her if she doesn't want to. She clearly is offended by your order."

Callista forced her features to remain impassive. "I do what is needed of me. Whether that is sharing my blood or spilling it. Come along, vampire. I do not have all day."

The chuckle that came from of the vampire made Callista want to return the grin that curved his lips. She shoved her arm further into the cage, felt the magics of the cage crawl along her skin, pulling at the frayed strings of the magics that kept her emotions in check.

The vampire strode forward, taking her wrist with a gentleness that surprised Callista. She expected him to grab her, gorge himself on her blood, and then toss her aside, and yet, this vampire grazed his thumb along her pulse, then lifted his eyes to clash with hers.

"If I had my powers, I'd make it more pleasurable for you. Have you ever been tasted before?"

Callista didn't answer him, simply glared, thankful for the magics that masked the sudden way her heart raced, the way her blood seemed to ignite under her flesh. She could not drag her gaze away as the vampire lifted her wrist to his mouth, cool lips on her skin, emotions threatening to unravel as she felt his tongue lick over her pulse.

Unable to hold back the gasp when the vampire's fangs pierced her skin, Callista felt the first pull of blood from her and her stomach turned queasy. Dragging her gaze from where the vampire groaned, shifting closer to the bars as if he wanted to get closer to her, Callista focused on a point on the wall and tried not to think about the fact that the vampire was drinking from her.

Or wonder why she was not as repulsed as she expected to be.

Vindicta nodded, then left them alone for a moment as Dylan continued to swallow her blood, then her gaze came back to his as his tongue lapped at the puncture wounds to close them. Callista snatched her hand back, rolling back down her sleeve. She took a shaky few steps toward the wall, her hellhound whining next to her.

Callista ran her fingers through her coarse hair, trying to settle her. "I am well Lagertha. Be at ease."

The vampire in the cage, who had been in the process of

licking the blood from his lips paused to look at her. "You named your hellhound after a shieldmaiden?"

Callista ignored the vampire as Vindicta came back in and the tension returned to the room.

"Good. You're done." Vindicta pulled out his ceremonial knife, with a blade that was forged in the very pits of hell itself and contained magics no one Inferna should wield. Striding to the cage, Vindicta used his magic to pull Dylan toward the bars. "Give me your hand."

"What are you doing?"

Vindicta smirked, glancing towards Scarlett. "Making sure you do not try and double-cross me. Or try and use this reprieve to formulate a rescue attempt. I will bind you to Callista so that she can track you if you try anything. I have witnessed that it is not all that pleasant to have your limbs ripped apart by hellhound teeth."

"I don't want any fucking part of whatever magics you've stolen. You'll have to trust my word."

Callista watched the exchange with interest as she waited for Vindicta to respond.

"I have not trusted a word from anyone since you all betrayed me and left me for dead. Give me your hand or I will start making the succubus bleed."

To punctuate his intentions, Callista watched as his fingers twitched and Scarlett let loose a cry of pain, a cut appearing on her chest just above her breasts. Dylan snarled, but he shoved his hand at Vindicta, who then slashed the blade along the palm of the vampire. Callista tried not to breathe as Vindicta called her over, repeating the action with her.

Then he placed their palms together, the sting of the magic causing both her and the vampire to snarl, Vindicta's hand placed over their joined palms as he muttered a spell and Callista wondered would there ever be a time when greedy men did not bind her in order to control her.

When the spell was done, Callista snatched her hand

away, letting Lagertha lick the blood until the wound was healed. It did not surprise her that the vampire licked the blood on his hands, winking at her when he caught her watching him.

"Tomorrow night, I will release you to go and get the pages of Lucifer's book and return them to me. Callista will go with you."

"Hell no," the vampire said, rolling his shoulders. "It's gonna be hard enough sneaking my fine ass into Sicarius without trying to sneak in your pet who has as much of a bounty on her head as you do. They will kill her on sight."

That statement was a strange comfort to her.

It tasted like freedom.

"Callista goes with you to make sure you return. It is my collateral."

"You have enough collateral in this fucking cage with me. I would never jeopardize her safety and you bloody know it, Dante. Letting me go alone is the smarter move. Your harpy looks like she wants to kill me herself. What's to stop her from trying and failing to kill me and ruin your plans?"

It was on the tip of her tongue to retort back to the vampire, tell him that if she wanted him dead, he was not strong enough to stop her, but Vindicta's eyes on her stopped the words from coming out of her mouth. Replying to Dylan would only betray the fact that the magics that held her emotions in check were beginning to come apart and that would mean Vindicta would try and reset it.

She could still hear her own screams of sheer agony from the last time Vindicta had taken away her human emotions.

Force of will and determination were all that held her in check as Vindicta cupped her cheek, his eyes on the vampire, who was glaring at the interaction. "Callista would not defy my orders. She is loyal. If I tell her not to kill you, she would not. If I told her to fuck you, she would."

Vindicta's grip became almost bruising as he gripped her

chin, his dark eyes holding hers. "Would you like to rut with my brother, Callista? I know how much Harpies enjoy fucking various Inferna."

Callista felt her talons wanting to get out as she coolly replied. "I'd prefer to gut him from throat to navel. I bet his insides would look better on the floor."

That seemed to please Vindicta because he released her, then turned back to Dylan. "Seems like there is at least one creature on this earth that does not want to get naked for you."

Dylan shrugged his broad shoulders. "Shit happens. Not everyone can have good taste."

Vindicta didn't respond to his brother, simply told Callista to ready herself to leave tomorrow night and to get the succubus some food. The moment Vindicta left the room, the pregnant succubus, Scarlett, sagged in relief. Striding around to her side of the cage, Callista crouched down, mindful that the vampire was keeping a close eye on her.

The hellhound stuck her nose into the cage, whining slightly, the succubus reaching out gingerly to rub along her long muzzle. It surprised Callista that as terrified as she was, Scarlett would still be brave enough to rub a hellhound.

"I didn't expect her to be so friendly." The succubus offered, those kind eyes of hers looking up at Callista.

"She can sense the child in your womb. As a mother herself, Lagertha knows the importance of keeping a pup safe. May I get you something to eat? You must be hungry."

Scarlett nodded, wetting her lips. "Thank you."

Callista rose and stood straight. "Lagertha will stay with you when we go to retrieve the pages. She will let no harm befall you."

The vampire was staring at her, his intense blue-green eyes held an intelligence that was masked by flippant remarks and sarcasm. Callista held his gaze, not backing down from the challenge even as her eyes burned.

"Dylan. Leave her be."

Scarlett's voice dragged her gaze from the vampire's and she almost cursed because of it. When Callista turned back to Dylan, he was still glaring at her.

"What?" Callista hadn't intended to ask the question, and if the vampire was not in the cage, she would have assumed that he was trying to use his empathic gifts on her.

"I'm trying to figure you out." He admitted, coming closer to the bars. "You want to gut me one minute, then you want to leave a hellhound to protect Scarlett. You could obviously claw Dante's rotten heart from his chest but you let him order you about. Tell me what I'm missing, Blue, cause I can't fit the pieces together."

Blue...

Over the past year surveying the Kiss and their mates, Callista had learned that Dylan, who also ran the assassin network, liked to give people nicknames, especially those within the assassin network. Keeva Cross, Malakai Cavanagh's fiancé was known as Death, her touch enough to kill a man. Malakai Cavanagh was known as El Diablo, though he tended to only take a job if it appealed to him.

Jasmine Cavanagh was known as the Widow, for she went after wife beaters and murderers. Ezekiel Collins, a man who once was a man of Catholic faith, was known as the Monk and he took marks on vile monsters who liked to harm children. The vampire within her grasp was simply known as Mac, and she knew that he normally gave into carnal urges after a kill.

Callista had watched the women and men who welcomed the vampire's touch, and while the rutting had never appealed to her, she did wonder if she might enjoy Dylan's touch.

"What just ran through your head, Blue?"

Callista must have frowned because Dylan smirked and drew in an exaggerated breath. "Your scent changed."

Horrified at her lapse of concentration, Callista gave Dylan a cold smile. "I was imagining how easy my blade would slide through your skin. I would peel the flesh from your bones and give them to my hounds as chew toys."

"If that's what turns you on, darling. But I don't think that's it."

Callista rolled her eyes, heading for the door when Dylan's voice stopped her.

"Answer me one question, Blue."

"Why should I even humour you, vampire?"

Dylan grinned, shrugging his shoulders. "I'm just trying to make sense of it all. You, Dante. This shitstorm we find ourselves in. One little question. I'll owe you a favour."

Callista knew that he was trying to charm her. He was handsome enough to know it, and still, here he was trying to use that against her. Had he not offered the favour in exchange for the answer, Callista would have walked from the room without looking back.

"Ask your question, vampire. I will remember you owe me a favour."

Dylan pressed his face against the bars. "Why do you stay and help him? Why take his orders and hurt innocent people when you could help stop him? Why don't you just leave?"

Callista considered his questions, considered arguing that he now owed her three favours. Instead, she reached out and grabbed the bars alongside where Dylan's fingers were, leaning in so that their faces were mere inches from each other. She could smell his scent, his sweat, and her stomach fluttered.

If she moved her head just a little, then her lips would be on his skin.

The thought sent her staggering back, shaking her head. She swallowed hard, praying that the vampire could not hear the way her heart galloped inside her chest. She had to give him an answer so that she could use the favour at a later time, but Callista felt suddenly tired, like her body was just weary.

Callista considered lying to the vampire, had the words already formed in her mind and yet, when she opened her mouth to reply, what came out was the most honest she had been to another Inferna in centuries.

"Sometimes, a person can be trapped within a cage, even if you do not see any bars."

It was a moment of madness revealing that sliver of herself to the vampire and from the way his brows lifted, the vampire had also not expected for her to reveal as much as she had.

Maybe it was the softening of his features, the hard suspiciousness that had been in his eyes the entire time he had been held captive seemed to ease, but then a look of understanding crossed over his expression.

Callista fled, forcing herself to walk away as if what she had said mattered little to her and it was but a passable remark. The sooner that she and the vampire retrieved the pages of the damn book Vindicta wanted the better.

She knew that Vindicta planned on killing Dylan rather than releasing him once the succubus gave birth, he planned on killing the entire Sicarius family. Once he had all of the instruments in place, Vindicta would proceed with his vengeance.

And yet, Callista would be glad when it was all over, when either good or the not so good prevailed. She just wished that the vampires knew the truth. That they knew all of the truth, even if she was spelled not to utter any inclination that might tell the vampires everything they needed to know.

Secrets had a way of making their way into the light of day, and like most secrets, like Callista herself, secrets would not stay caged forever. So, she would see it through to the bitter end, and try to keep from exposing herself any further to a vampire who could undo everything she had forged for herself.

She could not go back to being the harpy who had wept because her mother was disappointed in her. She would not return to being overwhelmed by emotions she was not supposed to bear. And that is what she told herself as she locked herself away in her chambers, sliding down the door as she sucked in a breath.

Callista did not understand why her hands were trembling, why her stomach felt nauseous, why she could not steady the racing of her heart. Perhaps she should have told Vindicta that the magics concealing her emotions was slipping.

Had he not been so consumed with the final stages of his mad plan, then he might have noticed. Then again, it was best he didn't.

"Sometimes, a person can be trapped within a cage, even if you do not see any bars."

Perhaps it was time to rattle the bars of her cage.

CHAPTER THREE

Dylan

DYLAN STOOD STARING AFTER THE HARPY WHO HAD WALKED away like she had not uttered the most sense with one little sentence, as if she had peered inside his very soul and summed up the feelings he had tried to keep hidden for so long. Callista had seemed so sad when she hinted that she too was a prisoner of Dante's. He hadn't needed his powers to feel the honesty in Callista when she spoke and yet, he knew from the power he had tasted in her blood that she was more powerful than he previously thought.

His head was still buzzing from tasting the harpy, his body hardening, and Dylan tried to convince himself that he was just feeling the after-effects from the blood lust and finally getting to feed. He would continue to deny it, yet, thanks to Dante's magical cage, the only emotions inside his head right now were his own, and despite the fact Callista was the enemy, he couldn't help being attracted to her.

"You like her."

Dylan shook his head and swallowed hard before shifting his gaze to Scarlett. "Even I'm not that much of a sexual deviant to want to fuck the enemy. Besides, you don't have your powers."

Scarlett laughed, a husky sound as she rubbed her belly. "I don't need my powers to see what's right in front of my eyes. You can be quite charming when you want to be, Dylan. Use that."

Dylan narrowed his gaze at Scarlett. "Are you really asking me to seduce the harpy, who has talons that could slice me to pieces?"

"Something tells me you'd quite like it."

That made Dylan laugh as he slid down beside Scarlett, ignoring the hellhound outside the cage. "And here I thought Keeva was the blood-thirsty one."

Scarlett nudged him with her shoulder. "I learned from the best. And I would do anything to get the hell out of here and make sure that monster doesn't get his hands on my baby. I'd seduce her myself, but I think she prefers blonds."

They fell into a comfortable silence, with Scarlett resting her head against his shoulder, her breathing changing as she drifted off to sleep. Dylan closed his own eyes, letting the blood he'd consumed settle into his veins, and now that he was not almost mad with hunger he could relax and try and formulate a plan.

Dante held all the cards here, but Dylan would try and find a way to figure out how to get Scarlett out of this cage. He wasn't overly concerned about his own safety. He could handle himself and he could handle the harpy. It was Dante that was the unknown, the wildcard in this whole fucking sorry mess and he wasn't sure what other tricks his brother had up his sleeve.

It reminded him of a time long ago, when they had all been made into vampires, and before Jasmine had found them again when they were still newly created and balancing the line between their hunger and their powers. Dylan had been driven almost crazy by the emotions of others, while Malakai had barely mastered his ability to read the minds of others. Dante, he was still furious that becoming a vampire had not given him any semblance of power and he constantly sought to become what he had not been in his human life.

"He must know more, Malakai. Delve deeper into his mind!"

It was an order not a request from their oldest brother, and

Malakai snarled at the blunt words. A reckoning had been coming for months now between the two when it started to become obvious that Malakai's powers and his strength as a vampire had accelerated. Malakai's vampire nature did not like to be given orders and Dylan felt the wave of violence ripple through Malakai even if his expression remained ice cold.

"If I go any further, Dante, I will break his mind."

Dante growled, taking a menacing step toward Malakai, and Dylan felt like his chest was going to rip apart at the aggression that was flooding his own veins, both his brothers' emotions seeping into Dylan and he gripped his chest to try and reign it in.

But it was futile.

"He knows where the leader of his Kiss is. We can avenge our village. We can take over and rule the very vampires who slaughtered our kin. We will have power and glory."

Malakai glared at Dante. "I already have power, Dante. I do not wish to lead. And forgive me brother, but you are not strong enough yet to take over an entire Kiss. Trying to do so would be certain death. One you would not come back from."

Dante's fury sent Dylan into a spiral and he surged forward, needing, wanting, bloodshed. Pulling a dagger from his waist, Dylan stabbed the gold right through the captured vampire's heart and then watched as the vampire disintegrated to ash as Dante let loose a frustrated scream.

"What the fuck, Dylan!"

Dylan wiped the blade off of his pants, then sheathed it, anger still rippling inside him. "Kai is right, Dante. We are bottom of the food chain right now. We need to take the time to grow in strength, and then we can kill our maker."

Reaching out with his power, Dylan tried to ease some of Dante's wayward emotions, the anger at having no magic, the jealousy of Malakai's growing powers, the bitterness that was etching into his soul, and when Dylan reached for Dante, his brother reared back out of his grasp.

"Don't you dare, Dylan. Don't use your powers on me."

Dante whirled round stalking through the forest, and then he vanished from sight. Dylan sagged in relief at the abrupt exit, and the fact he could barely feel Dante's emotions. What had happened to the brother who had trained both him and Malakai how to hunt, how to wield a sword? What had happened to the brother who liked to stay up all night and tell them stories of bards and warriors, kings and queens.

Dylan had always been aware of other people's emotions, and when Dante, who was a couple of years older than they were was made aware that all three of his siblings had powers and not him, the brother that once cared deeply for them had begun to resent them, especially Jasmine, who had followed Dante around the village.

A hand landed on his shoulder and Dylan glanced back at Malakai. "Let him go, Dylan. Perhaps tonight is the night we must part ways and let Dante find his own way."

Dylan opened his eyes with a sigh, peering down to see Scarlett still asleep in the crook of his arm. Of course, Malakai had been right about Dante. He had used the time away from them to band together his own Kiss and they heard tales of the bloodshed across Europe. He and Malakai had remained in Ireland, looking for any word of Jasmine, honing their own powers and they had not seen Dante for decades.

Footsteps sounded down the hall and Dylan inhaled a breath, recognising the cold, frosty scent of the harpy as the door opened and she stepped inside carrying a tray. Callista had showered and changed into clothes that screamed battle ready. Her blue hair was pulled back into a ponytail that gave Dylan a perfect view of her face. There was a harsh scar down her left eye that looked like a claw mark, and a glamour concealed the pointed ears he knew were there

Callista glanced at Scarlett sleeping, then at Dylan. "She must trust you immensely to sleep so soundly."

"How well do you sleep with my brother?" Dylan threw at her, noting the way her jaw clenched.

"I do not sleep, not with Vindicta and not by myself."

Dylan kept his expression blank so Callista would not know that he was curious about her. He also noted how she never called his brother Dante, only Vindicta. It was something that might normally have slipped his notice, but something told him it was information he needed to file away to use later on.

Callista walked around the cage to the side that Scarlett was on, the succubus' eyes fluttering as if the smell of the food lured her from her slumber. She stretched, then let her gaze drop to the bread and soup that Callista was holding. Dylan studied her as Callista dipped a piece of bread into the soup and then ate it, washing it down with some of the water on the tray.

She slid the tray inside the little hatch so Scarlett could take it, the succubus offering her thanks, then Callista rose and began to head for the door.

"Hey, what about me?" Dylan asked as he shoved to his feet and leaned against the bars.

The blue-haired harpy glanced down at her wrist, then lifted her green eyes to Dylan. "You have already fed, what else could you want to eat?"

Dylan smirked, letting a slow smile curve his lips. "I could think of one thing I'd like to eat."

Eyes narrowing like she was trying to figure out what Dylan was on about, Callista looked utterly confused even as Scarlett snorted out a laugh. Well, if the sexual innuendo wasn't going to work with the harpy he would just have to try and seduce her another way.

More footsteps sounded down the hall, a figure coming to stand in the doorway, his face guarded as he stepped further into the room, Lagertha growling at the new addition to this fucked up story, and Dylan couldn't hide the shock on his face as the assassin looked at Callista. "He's looking for you."

Callista inclined her head at the other man, brushing past

him, and leaving Dylan to glare at one of his own goddamn assassins.

"How long have you been playing both sides, Sniper?"

Ezra's eyes flashed amber. "I had no choice, Mac. He threatened my family. He threatened to torture those I love if I didn't do as he asked."

"So, you did it under duress, right? No money exchanged hands?"

The flush that darkened the other man's cheeks told Dylan all he needed to know.

"You son of a bitch. You tried to take out your squad leader. You were the one to take a shot at Roman."

Ezra snarled, shoving his hands into his pocket. "I didn't have a choice, Mac. I didn't have a fucking choice."

Dylan reached out and gripped the bars, pulling his face flush against the cold bespelled metal. "You always have a choice. Walk out the goddamn door and head straight to Sicarius and tell Roman what you've done and tell him where we are."

Ezra shifted uncomfortably at the dead stare from Dylan, running his hand through his hair. "Your sister just had to mate with Roman, didn't she? She just had to drag us into your fucked up family feud."

Dylan wanted to rejoice that his sister had let Roman into her heart. His fierce, wild, soft-hearted sister had been hurt before, and he knew that she had been into Roman from the offset, but Jasmine had to realize that for herself. It wouldn't have been fair if he had interfered; even though he had tried to push Scarlett and Zeke in the right direction when they danced around one another.

Showing Ezra a flash of fangs, the werewolf's eyes blazing in response to the aggression, Dylan said. "I'm going to enjoy watching Roman tear you limb from limb. I'm going to savour each tear of flesh, every drop of blood, and every single scream. And if Roman can't do it, I'm gonna let Death have her way with you. I think she'd like to have a go with one of her fellow assassins who broke the code."

The code within the assassin community was simple; you didn't reveal anyone else's identity, and you didn't kill or attempt to kill any other assassin without hitting up the bosses with a valid justification, which was essentially him, Kai, and Jazz.

Callista stepped back into the room, then glanced at Ezra. "He wants you now. I would go. Vindicta does not seem in the best of moods."

Ezra turned and headed off down the darkened hall as Dylan shouted after him. "Enjoy your last few days of oxygen, Sniper. The grim reaper is coming for ya, you fucking traitor."

"The forest has claws and teeth to claim you. Scars and blood and bone. Beware the traitor in your midst. It is those you least expect who will stab you in the front."

Shit, that was what Jasmine had predicted, a traitor hiding in plain sight. If he managed to get a message to his siblings about what was happening, then he would have to let them know all about Ezra.

Dylan felt eyes on him, as he turned his attention back to the blue- haired harpy studying him. He was about to say something, when Dante appeared over Callista's shoulder and placed a scarred hand on her shoulder, a wave of jealously rolling in his stomach.

He cursed himself that the emotion must have crossed over his face, because Dante trailed a finger down the curve of Callista's neck, a sickening grin on his face. Callista stayed ramrod straight, her eyes almost vacant, the tiny tick of muscle in her clenched jaw the only reaction to Dante touching her.

"Do you know that Callista has been in my employ since she was nothing but a rabid harpy about to be cast out of her Nest? I purchased her from her mother when she was a teenager. You see, she is half human, thus her mother thought she was tainted and so she sold her to me. I own her, and she will do anything I command. What a treat it was to find her in a market in Greece, a harpy who commands a pack of hellhounds."

Dante was staking his claim, showing Dylan that he had found the power he had been searching for long before Dante had been reborn as a vampire. His brother cupped the back of Callista's neck, leaned in to take a sniff, and Dylan wanted to surge forward and order Dante to let her go.

But that was the reaction that Dante wanted, so Dylan laughed and shook his head. "Dante, bro, you might have your Princess of hellhounds, but we have Death on our side. We have a succubus with more power in her little finger than you will ever have, even with all that stolen juice ravaging your body. We have Jazz, and we have Malakai, and if I was not in this cage, if you didn't have Scarlett as a prisoner, I would flood you with so much emotion that it would bring you to your knees in floods of tears. So, keep waving your dick around to try and prove that it's bigger than ours, but I guarantee you, in a fair fucking fight, you don't stand a chance."

Dante lost his composure then, shoving Callista away so hard she smacked her head against the stone wall, the coppery scent of her blood filling his nose as Dante held out his hand like he wanted to choke Dylan, lifting him off his feet as black filled Dante's eyes.

"Do you have any idea who I am? I will bend and break you, vampire. You have no idea what is coming, no clue" Dylan felt pressure at his throat as the black bled from Dante's eyes and confusion narrowed his gaze. "Dylan?"

The black returned and then Dylan was crashing against the bars, pain searing his back as he groaned and Scarlett rushed over to him. Magic pulsed in the cell and then Dante was storming from the room, his snarl of frustration echoing.

Dylan slowly got to his feet, wondering what the hell was going on. Why did Dante seem confused that Dylan was standing in the room with him? Maybe Callista would have answers for him. Dylan looked over to where the harpy was holding her sleeve up to her forehead.

"Are you okay?" Dylan asked Callista and she seemed to startle, like no one had asked her that question in a long time.

"Yes. It is not the first time I have been injured."

Scarlett had gone back to setting down, her hand through the bars rubbing the fur of the hellhound. Dylan strode over to the bars and beckoned Callista forward. "Let me have a look."

"It will be fine."

Her tone was clipped but he could scent the blood still, and knew the cut had to be deep. When Dylan shrugged and lifted a brow, Callista huffed out a breath like she was just humouring him. She removed her arm from the wound, blood still seeping from the gash that made Dylan want another taste of her. And yet, unlike Dante, he wouldn't touch her without permission.

"I can seal it. May I?"

The harpy seemed taken aback that he would ask for permission, but she took a step closer to the bars, lifted her head and closed her eyes. For one moment, Dylan considered that Callista was vulnerable in this position, that he could reach out and snap her neck in a split second and that would enrage Dante.

Dylan pushed the thought from his mind, leaning in to flick his tongue along the trail of blood, his cock hardening at the little involuntary shiver that caused Callista's body to tremble. Then Dylan sealed his lips over the cut and licked the wound closed. He almost startled when Callista's hand snapped out and gripped the front of his tee.

Lifting his mouth from Callista's cool skin, he glanced down to see her green eyes watching him and Dylan really wanted to know exactly what was running through her head. Her tongue slid out to wet her lips and dammit if Dylan didn't want to capture those lips with his own.

Callista must have read that in his eyes because she jerked back, letting go of his tee.

"What happened to Dante just now?" he asked, before the harpy could run away again.

She shook her head, strands of blue hair falling over her face. "I cannot."

"Can't or won't?" Dylan ventured, licking his own lips, feeling smug when Callista swallowed hard. Dylan thought she wouldn't answer him as she walked away and if he had not had supernatural hearing, he wouldn't have heard her whisper 'I cannot.' Before she disappeared from view.

CHAPTER FOUR

Callista

CALLISTA HAD BEEN RIGHT IN THINKING THAT THE MAGIC THAT Vindicta used to imprison her emotions was failing. She had let the vampire heal her wound because she felt compelled to do so. It had spread a warmth all along her skin the moment his tongue had lapped at the blood, and it had made her grasp his t-shirt, as if she was trying to hold him in place and not sever the moment.

And she did not even have the excuse of blaming it on the empathetic vampire's powers. No, it had been all her own actions, ones she would have to try not to replicate when alone again with the vampire. It wasn't hard for Callista to consider that her time spent spying on the Sicarius vampires had led her to feeling a little melancholy for the fact that all she had ever wanted as a young harpy was for her mother to show her any kind of affection.

But that was not the harpy way, and Callista had watched as the vampire siblings and their mates, showed their affection so openly, and so candidly. She had spent nights simply watching them interact, watching the touches, the kisses, the simple graze of fingers resting on an arm in comfort.

In truth, it was Dylan she had watched more than any of the others. It fascinated her that the vampire could one minute go from laughing with lots of people around him, to sitting in his darkened bedroom, his head in his hands and tears staining his face. How he could smile at any woman or man, ones only too happy to shed their clothes to have him caress their bare skin, and then once the rutting was over, to have this emptiness in his eyes.

The most Vindicta had touched her in years was yesterday in his attempts to gain an advantage over his brother, and in doing so, he had almost been the one to reveal the full extent of the cost of the magics burning away at his humanity.

It was a blessing, Callista supposed, that Vindicta was not one of those monsters who preyed on children, nor seemed to have any interest in her as a female. Indeed, it had been a long time since he had shown any interest in any woman.

Callista fastened her high-necked blouse and then proceeded to slip her arm braces over her wrists, the metal encircling midway up her arms. She slid her sword into the sheath strapped at her back, then slipped on her weapons belt containing various blades and daggers. Her legs were encased in black leather boots that went part ways up her calves, but were easy to manoeuvre in.

She had already been given her orders by Vindicta that afternoon so she doubted she would see him prior to the outcome of the mission. Her job was to make sure Dylan gets inside Sicarius Security to retrieve the pages and kill anyone who gets in their way. And yet, he had warned her against killing the obscurum, that Ezekiel Collins was still part of his plan, a part that Vindicta had not shared with her.

And why would he? For she was a mere tool that Vindicta wielded.

WHITE HOT RAGE seared through her and Callista had to close her eyes and steady her breathing and heartrate before she faced the vampire who made her feel things that threatened to shatter all her control. Lagertha's pups whined as they circled her, her emotions unnerving them.

"I am fine. I will be fine."

Callista gave the pups a rub and then she left them in her rooms, knowing she could summon them with a mere thought if she needed them. When Vindicta had told Dylan that she could command the hellhounds, it made her sound like it was a power she possessed and not a hard-earned trust between Lagertha and herself.

Truth be told, Callista had rescued the heavily pregnant hellhound from a market not quite unlike the one she had been sold from. The hellhound was being held in a cage, a small one that was cramped, with lots of bids for the hellhound who tried to maim any creature that tried to put hands on her.

The marketplace stank of magic and Inferna, the bustling streets filled with those who wanted to procure items that you could not find in a reputable place. The marketplace shifted every night, a new city, a new country, and only those who delved within the Inferna underbelly were privy to the location. Tonight the market was in Barcelona's long winding streets, and the balmy heat reminded her of the sunshine in her homeland of Greece.

Callista tried not to dwell on the fact that she should or could kill most of the vile cretins if she so wished, but she was not here for a massacre. No, she was here to pick up a package for Vindicta, who would not be best pleased if she returned without his package and if she had killed the Inferna who could help him fulfil his plan.

Most Inferna stepped aside as she strode down the busy street, listening to the cat calls and offers of everything from a night of passion to a power-magnifying spell. But it was the loudest yell of all, and the resounding growl that snared her attention.

Turning down one of the narrow side streets, Callista pushed through the gathered crowd to the front as she almost snarled at the state of the pregnant hellhound held captive in the cage. The hellhound lifted her gaze, black eyes like coal clashed with hers, and Callista could almost hear the plea for aid.

A warlock was bartering with the demon selling the hellhound for a price, and Callista knew that the warlock would use the hell-

hound in their spells, the blood in the hellhounds as powerful as the ichor of hell where they had once been created. The hounds would be cut down, killed for the power it would give the warlocks for their spells.

The warlock was offering the firstborn child of an Egyptian Princess when Callista shoved him aside and told the demon. "The hellhound is mine."

The demon scoffed at her, running his gaze over her with a sneer. "Go away, harpy. This does not concern little girls."

The gathered crowd snickered, the laughter fuelling Callista as she withdrew a dagger lightning quick, that was blessed with holy water, and plunged it right into the demon's eye She yanked it back out as the demon howled, his eye sizzling as the power of the blade crept along his skin, and he burst into flames.

The dagger would not kill the demon, but it would send him back to hell, weakened, and unable to claw his way out for maybe a couple of decades. Callista glanced at the crowd, arching a brow as if daring someone else to step forward and take her on.

Instead, they dispersed, leaving Callista to open the cage, cautiously, and probably stupidly reaching inside to place her hand on the enormous hellhound muzzle.

"You are free now. No one will imprison you again."

Callista had coaxed the hound out of the cage, the beast stretching to her full height, standing just shy of Callista's chest. She wasn't sure what she was to do now with the hellhound, but when Callista continued on her mission, the hound had followed her, and not left her side since then.

By the time she had shaken away her memories, Callista had reached the room where the vampire and the succubus were being held captive. The succubus was wide awake, but the vampire looked like he was sleeping, his head resting on top of his knees, his long blond hair covering his handsome face.

Callista turned to Scarlett, remembering their first face-to-face meeting. She hadn't needed to get so close to her, in the bathroom of the nightclub named after the brother they thought to have died centuries ago. Scarlett had smiled at her, and complimented her hair, her voice kind and friendly, unlike the lies Vindicta had told her about his family. She had let herself be swayed against Scarlett for being a succubus, a whore in the eyes of the Inferna, and yet, Scarlett had never been anything but nice to her.

"I'm not sure I like it when you look at me like I'm something you'd like to kill."

Scarlett's voice dragged her from her thoughts. "It may not seem like it, but I wish you no ill will. I was just reminded of how …nice …you were to me when we first met."

"You mean when you blew some magic powder in my face and made me horny as all hell?"

Callista shrugged and that made the succubus chuckle, then she glanced at Dylan before turning her bright blue gaze on Callista. "I might be a zillion months pregnant, powerless, and a prisoner, but I will hurt you if you hurt any of my family. I think you don't want any of this. I think you don't want to be a weapon. Keeva was once a monster's plaything; I can see it in your eyes. We can help you."

The vampire stirred, stretched with a yawn, preventing Callista from having to answer her.

"What I miss?" Dylan yawned again, rubbing sleep from his eyes, giving the impression he was still half asleep, yet Callista could see the sharp awareness in his eyes that told her differently.

"We are to leave." Callista said, coming forward to use the spelled key to unlock the cage, pausing as she glanced at Scarlett. "Would you prefer Lagertha to stay in the cage with you? She does not like it, but she will stay with you, if I ask it of her."

Scarlett shook her head. "No. I couldn't stand it if she was hurt because of me. It's okay."

Callista respected the succubus more than ever.

Turning her attention to the biggest threat, the key still not turned in the lock. "Do not force me to hurt you, vampire."

Dylan held up three fingers. "Scouts honour. I will be on my best behaviour. Unless you'd like me to misbehave."

Callista understood what the vampire was trying to, what was it the humans called it, ...flirt with her, lure her into a false sense of security. It meant nothing to him to try and use his charm on her, yet, it seemed like a waste of effort.

Turning the key in the lock, Callista pulled the door open and waited, ready to fight if Dylan rushed her. Instead, she watched as Dylan crouched down and embraced the succubus.

"You keep my niece in there until I get back if you can. I'll try not to be too long."

"If Zeke finds out he'll try and kill you." Scarlett warned Dylan.

"I can handle the old man. It's more your sister I'm worried about. I was sick as fuck the last time she tested her power on me. I'd prefer not to do that again."

Dylan hugged her tighter, then let Scarlett go, rising to his feet and turning to face Callista. "We can't go out to the streets just yet. The team will have drones and satellites scanning for any signs of me or Scarlett."

Callista rolled her eyes and sighed. "That is why we will go down, vampire." Stepping back, Callista motioned for him to come out of the cage, and she was perplexed when he hesitated. She assumed it was because of Scarlett, then he walked out, his expression guarded as if he was waiting for a blow.

Callista locked the door, the key disintegrating in her hand as she felt Dylan's magic pulse from him, and every single wall she had erected inside of her mind flew up. His gaze narrowed, and she steadied herself against his powerful gift.

"You really don't have any emotions, do you?" He asked, his curiosity open and honest on his face.

"It is a blessing."

"Some might say it's a curse."

Callista snorted, walking out into the corridor and around the corner, Dylan following after her. "I have seen the way emotion can cripple you, vampire. Would you say it is better to feel too much or not feel anything at all?"

Her words were snapped out and Callista cursed herself for another slip of restraint. She had shown Dylan another piece of who she really was and it did not bode well for the next few days and nights.

She expected him to pass a remark on what she had said, yet he seemed to hone in on another part completely.

"You been watching me, Blue? Is that what you like, eh? You like to watch?"

Callista ignored Dylan's rumble of laughter and the way it tightened her body, his laughter turning even louder, as he inhaled a breath. "Defo likes to watch."

Yanking open one of the doors, revealing the ladder down into the drains below, Callista was tempted to grab hold of Dylan and push him down into the sewerage below.

"You really want to push me down there, dontcha?"

Surprise must have flashed in her face because the vampire leaned in so that their noses almost touched. "I don't need to read your emotions to know when I'm getting under your skin."

Ignoring his comment, Callista simply stepped into the gap in the floor, freefalling until her feet hit the solidness of the concrete below, the stench tickling her nose, the rush of water alongside her and the screech of rodents a familiar sound.

She had a split second to jump out of the way before the vampire landed in a crouch, a rat running over his foot and he let loose a yell as he jerked back.

Callista snorted. "Afraid of a little rodent, vampire?"

"Hell ya. Especially when you wake up as a vampire and

there's one snacking on ya." Dylan shuddered, glancing around himself like he was trying to get his bearings.

Pointing to the most southern direction, Callista told Dylan. "That is the way to Sicarius. It will take you into the building across the river from your building. The drain will bring us under that building, and then we can discuss how to get inside."

Dylan whirled on her, glaring and she fought not to shirk back. "You're the one who fucking shot me with the arrow!"

"It wasn't a fatal shot." Callista said, holding his stare and not backing down.

"But it hurt like fucking hell, Blue."

"Again, I do not see the issue. It was not a fatal shot."

A rumble sounded in the vampire's chest, yet, Callista knew it was not a menacing growl, merely an annoyed one. She kept staring at him until his eyes flashed red, then he glanced away. "We can't go directly to Sicarius." He declared.

"Whyever not?"

Folding his arms across his broad chest, Dylan jerked his chin up. "For one, if you plan on sneaking into the most secure building in the world, it's best not to smell like a sewer when you do it. You might have been able to wash for the last few weeks, but I smell. I need to wash, feed, and come up with a way to distract everyone so that they get the hell out of the building so we go in and don't get interrupted.

"We do not have time for your vanity." Callista told him, shocked when Dylan stepped into her, his body almost flush against her.

"Take a sniff, Blue. Even the rats could smell me coming."

Callista tried very hard to not breathe in the scent of the vampire, her nose crinkling as she retreated. "You could have said all of this before we left. You could have washed before we left."

"Nah, then I wouldn't get the pleasure of your company while we come up with a plan."

And here he was again, trying to flirt with her.

"Where do you suggest we go to appease your vanity?"

Dylan rattled off an address in the opposite direction, but Callista knew there was a way out to the city almost under the building Dylan wanted her to go to. She headed down in the direction opposite to where the Sicarius building was, every instinct wanting her to glance over her shoulder at the vampire behind her, who was now whistling a tune as they walked.

"You know, you should feel honoured that I'm taking you to my place. Not even my own siblings know I have the loft. I don't invite just anyone to my private sanctuary."

"Perhaps it would feel more, honouring, if I had the capacity to feel."

There was a moment of utter silence then Dylan barked out a laugh. "Did you just make a joke, Blue?"

Callista didn't answer him, just stomped her way along the ledge of the drain, thankful that the darkness could mask her discomfort, a slip of her control letting her annoyance flare, as Dylan hissed and asked. "What was that? It happened so fast I didn't catch it."

"I have no clue what you mean, vampire. Hurry up. We are wasting moonlight."

The last thing she needed was to be stuck indoors with Dylan all day long as he sheltered from the sun. Held captive in a place where the vampire was comfortable, that he had not shown to anyone, not even his own family, would not do anything to stop from endearing the vampire to her.

Callista did not want Vindicta's plan to unfold any more than the Sicarius vampires did, but no matter the outcome, whether the door was opened, or Vindicta was defeated, Callista would be free. The magics that bound her to Vindicta, much like the magics that bound her to Dylan, was not an obvious thing; it simmered underneath her skin, ready to flare to life.

It would prevent her from talking about Vindicta to Dylan but it would also unleash her secrets should she become too complacent. She stole a glance over her shoulder to see the vampire watching her with intelligent blue-green eyes that sparkled when his lips tugged into a smile.

Callista snapped her head forward again as she realized that Vindicta was not the biggest threat to her freedom and her sanity; Dylan McGrath was.

CHAPTER FIVE

Dylan

FOR THE BRIEFEST OF MOMENTS, DYLAN WAS CERTAIN HE WAS able to pick up the spark of something coming from the harpy who claimed not to be able to feel a thing. The way his empathic powers worked meant that he knew how someone was feeling because he felt the same thing. There were times when he didn't know which emotions were his and which were ones that he was feeling from someone else.

In a crowded room, the weight of emotions used to threaten to cripple him, but now, after centuries, Dylan could filter through the emotions, when he wanted to. He wasn't proud of the fact that sometimes when his own emotions were confusing, he preferred to latch onto another person's feelings. He had slept with women and men, both human and Inferna, during his lifetime, because they had wanted him and Dylan didn't care enough about himself at the time to decide whether he himself wanted to have sex with them.

As he walked behind the blue-haired harpy with all her lush curves and powerful muscles, Dylan knew that he himself was attracted to her because when he reached out with his magic to try and discern any flicker of emotions, the feedback was like static. The darkness of the tunnel cast shadows against her features.

As if Callista felt the weight of his gaze on her, she glanced over her shoulder again, her lips pressed in a firm scowl as her brows narrowed before she pulled her eyes from his and stomped her way along the underground sewer.

Dylan was extremely intrigued by the fierce harpy who was working with his brother and it bugged the hell out of him. Malakai always told him that his curiosity would get him killed one day and many times over the years, his need to pull and pick at every little thing had landed him in trouble.

It was a miracle Malakai hadn't killed him by now.

Huffing out a breath, Dylan shook himself loose and then decided it would be best to use this time to try and get into Blue's head a little more. As curious as he was about the woman herself, Dylan was also curious as to what had happened to Dante last night, and the fact that Callista had been so quick to admit that she couldn't tell him what was going on with Dante.

When a wider ledge appeared up along, Dylan took the opportunity to get ahead of Callista, then walked backwards, facing her. "Since we are gonna be stuck together for the next while, maybe you can tell me more about you, Blue."

"No."

Her green eyes seemed luminous in the dark, as Dylan studied her, grinning at her curt response as he ran a hand through his hair as if he wasn't watching Callista for the slightest slip up, or searching for any weakness that would give him the upper hand.

"Come on, Callista. We can be friends, right?" He flashed her his biggest, sexiest smile, feeling almost saddened when she frowned.

"We are not friends, vampire. You are a tool I need in this moment. Do not be under any illusion that I would not separate your head from your neck if I had to. I am a harpy. All we are built for is dealing in death."

Dylan chuckled, shoving his hands in his pocket as he continued to walk backwards along the tunnel. "Now I'm sad, Blue. I was hoping we could end up friends. Hell, I'd offer you a job once we figure out how to kill Dante for good this time, if I thought you'd come work for me. I guess I'm down an assassin now because Roman will kill Ezra for his betrayal."

Callista's expression didn't so much as flicker as she walked and Dylan was pretty sure she was going to ignore him, then she opened her mouth to say something, then clamped it shut again. Dylan waited, giving her time because he knew if he pushed, the harpy might shut down and then he would get nowhere with her.

"You seem to like giving Inferna and assassins nicknames."

The words were said more as a statement than a question, as if her curiosity had gotten the better of her. And yet, for a creature who was supposed to be free of emotion, her question betrayed that sentiment.

"I hire assassins knowing their entire identity, but it's my job to make sure they are protected. And that works both ways. Any assassin who breaks the rules knows that I will come for them."

Callista tilted her head. "Rules?"

Dylan nodded, his expression going deadly. "Ya, rules. You agree to the rules when you take the job and then if you break them, you sign your own death warrant. No kids. No revealing another assassin's identity. No jobs taken unless sanctioned by Sicarius. Doing anything that might reveal the assassin network would result in death. No use of real identities during any meeting."

Callista looked like she was mulling over his rules when she inclined her head. "Is it true that you must verify that a person is being targeted justifiably before issuing a contract?"

Dylan nodded again. "Yup. We have a whole team who checks to make sure we do not target an innocent Inferna. We only kill monsters who threaten to reveal our world to the humans because of the horrific things they do. We might be assassins, darling, but we still have morals."

Callista walked in sync with him for a few minutes, looking like she wanted to say something more, and Dylan found that he was just as eager for her to say more. He liked the otherworldly sound of her voice, it was lyrical, like she had stepped into modern times from a place that was long ago forgotten.

Dylan and his siblings had evolved with the change of times. Their accents had changed to fit in with the time they were in. Kai never seemed to lose the air of authority when he spoke, whereas Jazz and he had submersed themselves in pop culture and music, sometimes sounding more like how they looked in age, then the centuries old vampires they were.

"How do you pick the nicknames?"

Dylan had to fight to keep his face serious, Callista's tone could only be described as eager, and again, it betrayed her insistence that she was emotionless. He paused, hoping his long wait to answer would make Callista show a sliver of the real her, ducking under a pipe that his vampire senses alerted him to. Then Dylan faced Callista again as he shrugged his shoulders.

"It depends on the skillset. Ezra was Sniper because he was a crack shot. Keeva was Death because she can kill you with her bare hands."

Callista ducked under the pipe, shielding her expression from him as Dylan heard her say. "I understand why you have called certain people certain names. Why are you just Mac?"

That question made Dylan grin, as he recalled the hilarious conversation with his family when they set up the assassin network. By telling Callista this, he was giving her a little sliver of himself but Dylan would do it, if it meant cracking that icy façade.

"That was all Jazz. We were just starting to update the

assassin network, and take on more so Malakai could concentrate on the more respectable aspect of Sicarius Security. While I've done my fair share of assassin jobs, I prefer the organizational aspect of it. It's hard to kill someone when their emotions literally overwhelm you."

Dylan watched as Callista studied him, but he grinned as he continued. "Jazz started saying I was like Charlie, from Charlie's Angels and that I should simply go as Mac, so everyone would know that Mac was in charge. The nickname stuck."

"Charlie's Angels?"

It hadn't dawned on Dylan that Callista might not understand the reference, and if Jazz was here, she would be grinning and interrupting by quoting Captain America: *I understood that reference.*

"It's an old TV show. Do you watch TV?"

Callista shook her head, a strand of her electric blue hair coming free from its ties. "Not a lot. We do not have a TV in the lair. I stayed in a hotel once and watched lots of Catfish. I did not realize humans could be so stupid."

Dylan snorted, laughing, and his reaction seemed to perplex the harpy because she pressed her lips tight together. It took him a second to realize that Callista didn't understand that he was laughing with her and not at her.

"You and Jazz with the bloody Catfish. Under different circumstances, you and Jazz would be friends, yano. You could mock the poor souls fooled because they are desperate for love while cleaning your favourite knives."

Callista's lips turned upward for a split second before she seemed to realize her slip, brushing past him, a small fraction of light catching her in the face and Dylan could see the look of panic that flashed over her features. Yet amazingly, Dylan could still feel no emotion coming from the harpy.

"Where is your family?" Dylan inquired, changing the subject and pretending that he hadn't noticed her lapse.

Callista shrugged, then rolled her shoulders. "At this moment, I assume that my mother and my sisters are in Greece. They were, last I heard, very well regarded within the Inferna in Greece. They do not like imperfection, they simply like to kill and to rut."

The harpy uttered the last part like she was equal parts envious and disgusted.

Dylan grinned, returning to walking backwards. "Well, considering those are two of my favourite things, I might get on well with the harpies." Dylan paused, holding Callista's icy glare before he continued. "Well, present company excluded it seems."

Callista sighed. "I have watched you enough to witness how much you enjoy the rutting. It is not something that appeals to me."

Dylan was so focused on the heat that surged through his body at the thought of Callista watching him fuck other people that he almost missed another slip from Callista. From what he knew of harpies, despite the lack of emotions, they had a veracious sexual appetite. That Callista said sex didn't appeal to her was another reason as to why Dylan thought the harpy was different than her kin.

"Maybe you just haven't had good sex. Maybe you need to just find someone that can make the sex enjoyable."

Callista halted her movements, tilting her head to the left as she regarded him. Dylan kept walking backwards, the grin that was on his face faltering when he heard Callista say, "Having not experienced the act for myself, I must assure you that from seeing others ...rutting... it is not something I feel the need to put myself through."

Dylan lost the rhythm of his steps and almost tripped over his own feet as he stumbled to a stop, lifting his wide eyes to Callista. "Wait...what? ... I'm not sure I heard you right. Are you telling me that you've never had sex?"

Callista's expression remained stony as she shrugged, then

shook her head. "No. I have never rutt- I have never had sex. I do not understand it, this need to join bodies together, sharing bodily fluids while making a mess."

So, the harpy was untouched, unclaimed by any other Inferna or human. He almost growled in satisfaction, something primal inside him seemed to awaken. Scarlett had suggested he seduce Callista, that he might enjoy it, and he would, Dylan knew he would, yet, he wanted to get in under her skin.

Dylan stalked towards her, watching as she retreated a step, then squared her shoulders and refused to budge when he crowded her. "But darling," Dylan started with a sensuous smile, "Making the mess is the best part. It's all about the touching, the tasting, the feel of someone shuddering because they liked what you did."

There was no way not to notice the hitch in her breathing, not to notice the slight parting of her lips and Dylan wanted to close the distance between them. But he restrained the urge to do just that because fucking her against the wall of a dirty sewer was not something Dylan was okay with.

Callista went as if she wanted to pass him by, her chin jutted out as she said with conviction. "Again, I do not see the point of it."

Dylan snapped out his hand, gripping Callista's arm as she went to pass by and they stood, side by side, shoulder to shoulder, facing one another, Callista glaring at him with a heat that shouldn't be possible from a heartless harpy.

"I think I can change your mind. I know I can."

It would take nothing to lean forward and capture her lips with his own, to see if a kiss could thaw the ice in her spine and see if the fire he suspected burned in the harpy's veins actually did. By the Gods, he had forgotten what it was like to want for himself, to crave something for himself.

"Unhand me, vampire."

"Make me, harpy."

Callista held his gaze defiantly for a couple of heartbeats, then she moved with a quickness that surprised Dylan, jerking her arm from his grasp and ducking under Dylan's arm before he could react, then strode away from him, leaving him standing open-mouthed and hella impressed.

They would get back to Callista's aversion to sex later, but they would be talking about it again. Hey, if he was going to die before the week was out then he wasn't going to miss the opportunity to get the harpy in his bed.

Callista kept moving, faster than the languid pace they had been setting before and Dylan had to jog to catch up to her.

"Nice move. You're super quick."

"I know." Came her tart response and Dylan liked it.

Silence descended upon them as they traipsed through the draining system, Callista letting out a snort when Dylan jumped when a rat scuttled along beside them. Dylan had meant it when he said that he had awoken as a vampire after days buried in the earth to have rodents chewing at his flesh. What he wasn't going to share with her was how he'd been so starved from bloodlust that he might have snacked on a few before clawing his way out of his grave.

When Dylan had finally dragged himself from the earth, it was to see Malakai tearing the throat of a young man, a farmer, who had the misfortune of passing through the field when Malakai had awoken. Malakai had snapped his gaze toward him, red in his eyes, blood just dripping down his chin. The hunger had roared in Dylan's stomach, burned in his throat and then he heard another heartbeat coming up on them and Dylan could hear the woman scream, the vibration of it tingling his fangs as he drank.

It was then his powers had woken up. When he was human, Dylan was able to persuade anyone to do what he wanted. He was able to make someone feel better with his presence. No matter the emotion, Dylan sensed it, but it was nothing like the torrent of emotions that he could now feel after becoming a vampire.

It had taken decades for him to get control over it and Malakai had made sure that they remained in sparsely populated areas whenever Dylan was overcome from the emotions of others. But Malakai worried, even if his expression didn't give it away, so Dylan worried then.

And then there was Dante. He and Malakai had been so lost in bloodlust when Dante had clawed his way out of the dirt that Dylan had felt the waves of rage coming from him. It had brought Dylan to his knees, clutching his chest with every step that Dante made in their direction.

When he discovered that both Malakai and Dylan had awoken with immense power and he had not, Dante had stormed off in search of blood and it had been months again before their paths had crossed.

Dylan and Malakai had gone back to their village in search of survivors, in search of Jasmine, but their sister was gone, presumed dead. It was not until Jasmine found them a decade later and forced Malakai to make her a vampire, that they knew she had not only survived, but had become a fierce warrior.

Fingers snapped in front of Dylan's face, jerking him to a halt, surprised that he had allowed himself to lose concentration when Callista could have gutted him a dozen times over.

There must be something seriously wrong with him because the thought only strengthened the attraction he was feeling towards the harpy.

"Pay attention, vampire."

Dylan shrugged, watching as Callista pointed up the ladder that seemed to have appeared out of nowhere.

"That will lead us up into the address you gave me. If this is a trap, Vindicta will gut your succubus. And I will claw out your family's hearts before they have a chance to strike at me."

Dylan folded his arms across his chest. "And here I thought we were becoming friends. No tricks, scout's honour. But there will be one, maybe two Sicarius employees up there and they are not involved in this. They are surveillance only, no one is trained to fight so leave them be."

Callista placed her hands on the ladder, then seemed to think better of it, motioning for Dylan to go up ahead of her. "I do not harm the defenceless. Just like you claim to have them, I have morals too. Now move."

Dylan climbed up the ladder, pausing on the fourth rung, then glanced over his shoulder at Callista. "I don't mind if you check out my ass, harpy. I'd actually really like it."

The growl that rumbled from the harpy in frustration had him laughing, which caused her to growl more. Dylan was still chuckling as he began to move again, and he couldn't help but think that this was the most fun he'd had in fucking ages.

CHAPTER SIX

Dylan

DYLAN PUSHED UP THE HATCH, BLINKING A FEW TIMES SO THAT his eyes adjusted to the sudden fluorescent lights. He held open the hatch for Callista, holding out his hand to help her up, but the harpy just glared at him like he'd offered to take her to a strip club.

With a sigh, Dylan let the hatch fall back into place, then opened the door and peeked out into the hallway. Callista had been right, the drains had brought them straight to his private residence, the place he went to escape from everyone and just have time to himself. In truth, he hadn't been here in a while with everything going on.

Before Dante started to mess with their heads, Dylan could disappear for days on end and his family would assume that he was off on a bender or something. Little did they know that he had stayed alone in his apartment and just tried to find some semblance of peace.

When Dylan was sure that there was no one else lingering in the halls, checking first for a heartbeat and then for emotions, he strode out into the hall and toward an elevator that had no buttons. He watched as Callista scanned the area, then seemed to search for buttons that Dylan knew were not there.

Dylan cleared his throat, and held a finger to his lips, earning a cocked brow from the harpy and then he grinned.

"Sicarius, initiate incognito mode."

"Incognito mode initiated."

Callista had withdrawn her sword and was braced for attack a moment later, and Dylan rolled his eyes. "It's the AI, the artificial intelligence that runs the Sicarius Security networks. I had to issue the command because no doubt, my number two Isolde would have set up an alarm for anyone trying to access the network and alerted the family to where I was."

Sheathing her sword along her spine once again, Callista nodded and Dylan waited a second before he continued.

"Sicarius, admit two Inferna to the penthouse. This is Callista. For now, she is a friend. Please use stealth mode when admitting us and alert me to any person trying to do a sweep for unauthorised access."

"Yes, Dylan. Please be aware that Isolde tried to bypass standard commands to set up an alert and there is a team scanning code for any anomalies."

"Thank you, Sicarius. Please alert me if they find out that I have accessed the network. We will head up now."

The doors to the elevator opened, and Dylan stood back to let Callista go first, but the stubborn Inferna refused so Dylan walked in and then Callista followed, putting herself flat against the wall so that she could watch the door and also keep a steely eye on him. The elevator whirred to life and they started their ascent.

"When did you learn about computers?"

The question surprised him, but Dylan leaned against the wall as he answered her honestly. "The problem with most Inferna is that they don't change as the world changes around them, whether it's technology, clothing etc. But Kai, he was adamant that we could only be successful if we flowed with the change. He sent me to college so that I could learn about technology and I enjoy it. So much so that I go back every few years to stay up to date with it."

Callista was watching him with that blank expression of

hers, but Dylan could see that she was eager to say more, so he bided his time, letting her patience wear out and was rewarded with another question.

"Yes, Inferna have become too complacent and stuck. We use swords still, and humans use guns. It was smart to be abreast of changes. Are you the only one who can override the system?"

"Are you asking because you're curious, or are you planning on torturing anyone who could get you into Sicarius without you needing to keep me alive?"

The harpy blinked in surprise, then placed her hands on her hips, making her look younger than her actual years. "I was merely curious, vampire. It would not be smart to leave the power in one mere Inferna's hands."

Dylan chuckled, and he watched as Callista rubbed her arms. "I dunno if I should be happy that you think I'm smart or insulted that you think I'm just a mere Inferna."

"I was refereeing to Malakai as the smart one. He is the leader of your Kiss."

Dylan barked out a laugh, shaking his head. "Damn, Blue. That's brutal. You're crushing my poor heart here."

"I'm sure."

Dylan was just about to challenge her again, enjoying the verbal table tennis a little more than he should, especially since the snippets of sarcasm were appearing more often, then the doors opened, and he stepped passed her into his safe space. It felt strange having her here, in his sanctuary, but there was something weirdly satisfying that he didn't even want to touch on because Dylan didn't want to consider what that might mean for him.

Callista strode into the kitchen area, then descended the steps to go down to the massive windows and gaze outside. The glint of the moonlight against her pale skin made her look almost angelic, ethereal, and maybe his harpy was exactly that, a goddess with a backbone of steel and a fierceness that called to him.

And when the fuck did he start thinking of her as being his?

Dylan cleared his throat, pointing to the double doors to his right. "Bedroom's in there. Bathroom too if you'd like to clean up. I have to go and speak to the staff that are here, but you can make yourself at home."

Callista had been already shaking her head the moment Dylan suggested they separate, the blue scar markings on her face seeming to glow. "We do not separate. I will go with you."

"Jesus, Blue. Anyone would think you don't trust me. I'm hurt."

Her gaze narrowed as she responded with another cutting remark. "Trust is earned, not freely given. I do not trust you. It goes against everything that you and your Kiss stand for not to seek aid from your family."

All Dylan could do in response was to shrug his shoulders and walk toward the bookcase that lined the wall to his left. Dylan skimmed his fingers along the spines of the books, aware that Callista was watching him. He reached for the spine of *Ulysses* by James Joyce and pulled it down.

There came a click, and then a whirl as the bookcase began to slide along the wall revealing a pathway that it had been concealing. Dylan snuck a glance over at Callista to see if she was impressed by it, but all he saw was a blank, unamused expression, and Dylan hated to admit that he was a little annoyed by her nonresponse.

"Come on." He grunted out, not waiting for her as he stalked down the darkened corridor, the sound of his footsteps like a hammer in his ears. He was acutely aware of Callista behind him as he clenched and unclenched his fists, perplexed at the suddenness of the anger in him. Dylan knew the anger was all his because he still couldn't pluck any sort of emotion from the harpy and the thick concrete that surrounded the little computer room from his residency was enough to block out the emotions of the team in there.

At this time of night, or early morning, there would be only one member working in the control room and it was easier that way. When they reached the end of the hall, Dylan glanced up at the tiny camera that angled in his direction. Dylan held up his middle finger, could almost hear Rob's laughter, and then the steel door opened.

They went into the computer room, the one that no one knew about, that was more connected to the Sicarius network than the ones at the headquarters. When he designed the programs he knew that if their home was compromised, there had to be a backup system that only a handful of people knew about.

It didn't look like much compared to the data centre that Dylan had at home, but this was as powerful as the other. When he had designed it, there had been an inside joke between him and the Inferna who was wheeling himself toward where Dylan stood, not to make it look like he was piloting a goddamn spaceship. So, Dylan had made sure it was built in the shape of something from Star Trek, complete with captain's chair and all that.

Rob had hated it.

Speaking of the man himself, the Inferna, a warlock whose magic worked on technology, Rob had been a soldier dealing in army communications when the truck he was traveling in hit a landmine and it shattered his spine. He was discharged from the army and had applied to Sicarius. Initially, Dylan hadn't hired him, but that was only a smokescreen. Dylan had wanted the talented computer whiz to work solely for him, off the books, and in turn, Dylan looked out for him and paid his medical bills. Isolde was the only person who knew Rob worked for him.

Despite his skills, it had taken Dylan some time to get

used to Rob's colourful use of language. The dark- haired man's face was almost red as he began to speak, and Dylan had to bite his lip not to burst out laughing.

"You cocksucking sonofabitch! Where da fuck have you been? Your entire fucking family has been going apeshit looking for you and the succubus!"

Dylan grinned, holding out his fist to bump Rob's. "And they'll still be looking for me. I need to stay under the radar for a while yet."

"Hades fucking testicles! I watched the Monk eviscerate a poor asshole and you tell me NOT to tell them your ass is alive and fucking kicking. Are you goddamn fucking insane, mate? Are you fucking certifiably insane?"

Dylan looked at Callista, whose eyes had widened at Rob's inability to verbalize a sentence without inserting a curse word. The moment Dylan's gaze shifted to Callista; Rob's head snapped in her direction.

"Who da fuck is that?"

Dylan inclined his head to Callista. "Rob, this is Callista. Callista, this is Rob, head of my personal security network and a gentleman when he's not swearing so much."

"Go fuck yourself, vampire." Rob said to him before tipping an imaginary hat at Callista. "Nice to meet ya…" Rob's eyebrows knitted together as he realized who she was. "Sonofawhorehouse…you're the blue-haired bitch that kidnapped him in the fucking first place."

Rob moved with a soldier's speed still, pulling a gun from the strap on the side of his chair and aiming it at Callista. He cocked the gun, his hands steady as Callista sighed, and glanced at Dylan, who just shrugged.

"Stand down, Rob. Callista and me are working together for now. Do you really think I would bring her here if I had a choice? Lower the weapon."

Rob kept the gun raised for another second or two, then lowered it. Dylan closed his eyes, sensing the man's unease and Dylan used his magic to ease some of that tension. Rob's shoulders relaxed, a serene expression on his face before he glared at Dylan.

"Don't use your fucking freaking zen shit on me, Dylan!"

Dylan shrugged, causing Rob to snarl, and spin around in his wheelchair as he grumbled. "How the fuck did you end up saddled with her?"

Opening his mouth to speak, Dylan was about to tell Rob exactly what had happened but all that came out was a jumble of words that made no sense. Dylan frowned, then tried again. "Car trolley pizza cat tea and sandpaper."

Rob glanced from Dylan to Callista and back again. "Was that supposed to make goddamn sense?"

Dylan snapped his gaze to Callista. "Why can't I tell him about …things?"

Callista leaned against the wall, resting her hands on her stomach. "Do you remember when you asked me if I would tell you what had happened with him and I told you I could not? It is because he bespelled me so that I cannot speak of him to anyone who has not seen him physically. When the blood bound you to me, the spell transferred to you also."

Well, that spoiled Dylan's plan to warn his family that Dante was back and a bigger pain in the ass than before. He had hoped that he could try and reach out to Kai or Jazz while they were trying to get inside Sicarius to get the pages. Now that plan was ashes in the wind.

"This is a fucktastrophy!" Rob exclaimed, shaking his head.

"That's not even a word, mate." Dylan replied, struggling not to laugh.

"Well, it fucking is now."

Dylan rolled his eyes, checking the time on the wall before he said. "We're gonna spend the day here, but make sure the rest of the crew don't try and alert anyone at headquarters. I'll need to shower and sleep and feed, but we should only need a day or two to get a plan together."

"Don't fucking die, you stupid sonofabitch."

Glancing at the warlock, Dylan grinned. "Awh, you worried about me, mate?"

Rob snorted as he turned his chair back toward his computer screens. "Fuck no. You're the dickhead that pays my wages. The HBIC might forget."

HBIC or head bitch in charge was what Rob called Isolde, the man having no sense of his own mortality by calling her that to her face, and his head of security did nothing more than pat Rob on his head.

Dylan headed out of the room, Callista falling into step beside him as the door closed, locking them out. They walked down the corridor, shoulders almost touching and although he sensed that Callista had something to say, the harpy remained tight-lipped until they exited the security area and Dylan had closed the secret passageway.

"We do not have much time to delay."

There was a strain in her voice, like the thought of being locked away with him alone for a few days was something akin to torture. Dylan ignored her, striding over to his fridge and pulling out a bottle of blood. He drained it, almost cringing at the bland taste of it. Nothing compared to the spark of fire that had ignited his veins the moment he had swallowed Callista's blood.

Tossing the bottle in the bin, Dylan pointed at the fridge. "There's food and stuff in there if you're hungry. I'm gonna take a shower and then get a few hours of proper sleep."

"We do not have time for this."

Dylan glanced out the window, then pressed a button that changed the tint on the windows that shielded him from the incoming sun. "The sun will rise in a few hours. There's not enough time to get to Sicarius, get the scrolls, and back before one of us catches on fire. If you don't want to sleep, the TV probably has episodes of Catfish to keep you entertained. Unless you want to shower with me and we can see if you'd still think getting naked isn't something that appeals to you."

The way the harpy's nostrils flared made Dylan think he had struck a nerve. Kicking off his shoes as he yanked his dirty t-shirt over his head, his jeans were next, and then he shoved the clothes in the washing machine, holding back his grin as Callista just stared at him.

Dylan knew he was handsome. He had always been but the way Callista was looking at him now, made him want to close the distance between them and fuck her on the floor. He wanted to sink his fangs into her throat so he could take her hard and fast, her blood surging through him.

Walking down the steps, dressed only in a pair of black boxer shorts, he did nothing to hide the fact that he was aroused, feeling Callista's eyes on him as he went into his bedroom. He left the door open, then pulled down his boxers, giving her a view of his bare ass. Then he went into the bathroom and straight into the shower.

Dylan stood under the spray, resting his palm against the cold tiles, his other hand wandering down to stroke his rock-hard erection. Closing his eyes, a growl rumbled in his chest as he pictured Callista in the shower with him, her hand around his shaft, stroking him to madness. He imaged her talons extending, fisting his cock so good, and the next thing Dylan knew he was coming, harder, and quicker than he had in years.

The harpy had managed to get under his skin, had managed to unnerve him. Dylan didn't want to think about what would happen when this was all over. Because even if they managed to defeat Dante, even if they managed to stop whatever dastardly plan he had, his family would never approve of him and Callista.

Washing himself off, Dylan snorted, opening his eyes, pulling the tie from his hair, and letting the long strands free.

He wasn't surprised to see dirt and blood going down the drain. What the hell was he even thinking that him and Callista could make it work? Even if his suspicions were right and the harpy wasn't as emotionless as she pretended, her being for him was something he couldn't even think about. Then deciding to claim her, deciding to …

It would mean that Dylan could never return to the family that he loved so fiercely with all his heart. It would be like he was being torn in two, his heart ripped apart, and he couldn't bear to be away from his family.

It was better this way, Dylan thought. His little crush was just that, a silly little crush that would disappear when he was back home where he was supposed to be and out of the harpy's proximity.

Well, that's what Dylan told himself as he shut off the shower, filled with more resolve than he had. He would stand beside his family and agree to whatever punishment they wanted to dole out for Callista's part in Dante's plan. He told himself that he would be fine with it, even as he tasted the lies in his own thoughts.

CHAPTER SEVEN

Callista

CALLISTA BUSIED HERSELF BY CHECKING THE FRIDGE TO SEE IF there was anything edible in it, but after staring at the contents for a few minutes, unable to get the image of the vampire naked out of her head, and the sound of the shower giving her all kinds of sensual images. Her mouth felt dry, and her skin too warm as Callista slammed the door to the fridge closed and walked back into the sitting area.

Dylan McGrath was dangerous to her self-preservation. She had no clue as to why she had divulged her aversion to sex to the vampire when she knew he seemed to enjoy the act. His partners also seemed to enjoy the act, their heady moans and groans had only punctuated the look of pure bliss on their faces.

It was not that Callista did not think Dylan was physically appealing, she had appreciated the toned muscles and rounded rear-end. It was the fact that if she succumbed to whatever pull she felt toward the vampire, that he could unravel her secrets and once the magics wore off this time, the ones that shielded her from Dylan's powers, there may not be a way to turn off her emotions again.

"Broken. My child is broken." Her mother spat on the ground, a look of disdain on her face as she regarded the other harpies in the Nest. *"It would be better to end her now. She will weaken us. I can almost hear her feelings."*

But her mother had not killed her. No. Instead, she had

caged Callista and offered her up to the Inferna world as if she mattered little to anyone. And that was what Callista thought happened to harpies and Inferna. It wasn't until Vindicta made her spend days and nights watching the Sicarius Security Kiss that she realized that what happened to her was not the norm.

Her bones felt suddenly weary and Callista sat down on the couch facing the window. Normally, she would not have dared remove her armour, but she did not need her weapons to protect herself. Slipping off her sword sheath, she lay her blade down beside her, then removed the leather cuffs at her wrists and shoulders.

Callista unbuttoned her vest and then shrugged it off, rolling up the sleeves of her tunic. White scars marred her skin, wounds inflicted by talons of her kin before her immortality had settled and her ability to heal became active. Unbinding her hair next, Callista let the blue strands cascade over her shoulders, then she shook it out.

Had she known that the retrieval of the pages would take longer than a few hours, Callista might have brought more provisions for the mission. Not that she was vain in the slightest and she knew that her face was not a face one would consider appealing.

It wasn't hard to see how Malakai Cavanagh had fallen for the banshee, Keeva Cross. Her features were unusual, and striking, a face that stood out in a crowd even when standing next to her best friend the succubus. Jasmine Cavanagh was even more attractive than the succubus, and Callista admired her ability to slip into whatever skin her environment required.

It was not a skill Callista had, the ability to shed who she was and become another person depending on her predicament. It was too hard for her to maintain the façade that she was unfeeling. After watching the vampires and their partners, Callista couldn't help but wonder what her life could have been like if she had not been sold to Vindicta but sold to someone like the Sicarius vampires.

"Hey, you want to eat before we get some sleep?"

The sound of Dylan's voice dragged her from her thoughts, and Callista bolted to her feet, braced to attack. Dylan held up his hands and Callista huffed out a breath. "You should not sneak up on creatures who can gut you with one hand."

Dylan came forward, and Callista could scent the body wash he had used, the lush intoxicating scent of his shampoo that made her want to close her eyes, inhale deeply through her nose and commit it to memory.

She was losing her mind...she was going crazy.

Dressed in lounge pants and no t-shirt, Callista scanned down the planes of his marble-cut abs and the V that pointed from his stomach to a part of his anatomy that had Callista's face heating again.

"I wasn't sneaking, Blue. You just looked like you'd zoned out. What were you thinking about?"

Callista watched as Dylan strode over to the fridge, pulled it open, and then took out a few items. Her stomach rumbled and she realized it had been a few days since she had eaten a proper meal. The kitchen and sitting area were separated by a bar, with stools on her side, so Callista sat down and leaned her elbows on the bar.

The vampire had taken out a frying pan, then he lifted those blue-green eyes that reminded Callista of the waters near where her birth had taken place, looking at her through thick lashes. "Anything you don't like to eat? I'm kinda limited as to what I can cook, but tell me if you don't eat bacon or eggs or hell, don't like toast."

Callista snorted, rolling her eyes. "What creature have you met that does not eat toast?"

Dylan cracked an egg, then grinned. "Nadeem. I know

he's like a sultan or some shit but he actually can't stand to eat toast for some reason."

"Ah the Prince of Whispers."

Dylan barked out a laugh and Callista felt pride swell in her chest. "Don't bloody tell him that, will ya. He'll be acting the langer putting that on a business card and everything."

Callista didn't say anything in response, wondering why the vampire was trying to engage in conversation with her, especially when she was essentially the enemy. He had let the fact that she had been the one to shoot him with the arrow go quite easily. She expected his retribution to be swift, and had prepared herself for it. Yet, she was not prepared for him to be so friendly.

Her lips pressed together in a firm line, and she must have let her features show her confusion because Dylan was looking at her, studying her, when she blinked her eyes to focus.

"What made you go all serious again?" He asked, flipping the eggs, then reaching around to put on the toast.

"Do you always ask this many questions?"

Dylan shrugged, plating her eggs and bacon then his own. "Well, normally I'd be able to feel what was wrong with you but since that's not going to happen, I have to ask."

Panic began to simmer in her blood. "Trying to garner feelings from me is useless. But since you asked and are feeding me, I will answer your question. I was wondering why you were being this pleasant to me when I am the enemy. If it was me, then I would be trying to exploit any weaknesses, and ensuring that my enemy was fed would not be the way to do it."

The toast popped, and Dylan piled that onto a plate, going back to the fridge for butter, asking Callista if she wanted water or juice, then poured her a glass of orange juice. Instead of taking a seat at her side of the bar, Dylan hoisted himself up on the counter, his own plate beside him as he lifted a piece of bacon and bit into it.

The vampire waited until Callista had taken a bite of her own bacon, using the fork Dylan had set out for her, then he spoke. "I don't think you're the enemy, Callista. Have you done some shitty stuff to me and my family? Did you almost have Keeva killed by a hellhound? Did you shoot me with a goddamn arrow, and did you help Dante kidnap me and Scarlett? Yeah, but I'm kinda hoping you are as much an unwilling participant as we are in Dante's plans."

Callista narrowed her gaze as she took a sip of her orange juice. "I did not send any hellhounds after Keeva. If anything, I should want to eviscerate your sister for killing one of my pups. They were sent to frighten but would have retreated at my call."

The growl that came from the vampire was inhuman. "You won't touch my sister. And I saw the damn hellhound. I don't know anyone else who has a pack of hounds so convince me it was not you."

Dropping her half-eaten piece of toast, Callista leaned back. "I am not the only Inferna who has the loyalty of hell-hounds. Hell, some Inferna have control over the beasts and train them to attack. You may not believe me, but it was Angus who branched out and sought the use of hellhounds to try and kill the banshee. I would not send my hounds to kill Death because I know not if her power works on them. I would not have them suffer."

Dylan shuddered, the fierceness in his features completely gone as he finished his food, then reached over and took her half-eaten toast from her plate, before popping it into his mouth. "As a recipient of Keeva's powers before, I don't blame you. I mean, it was something I'd not like to experience again."

"Your brother's mate hurt you?" The anger and disbelief

in her own tone surprised Callista, and from the widening of Dylan's eyes, it took him by surprise also.

"It was nothing," Dylan said with a sigh. "We realized that for some reason, Keeva's power didn't work on Malakai. Nor Jazz. Worked on me so we assume it had something to do with the fact Malakai and Jazz have the same mother and me and Jazz have the same father."

"You are not blood related to Malakai?" This was a snippet of information that Vindicta had not divulged to Callista, and he would have known this fact.

"Doesn't matter. He's my brother as much as Jasmine is my sister. It was the same with Dante. We had the same mother and he and Malakai have the same father."

Callista snorted, taking a forkful of egg before she swallowed and replied. "That is very confusing. With all the rutting and birthing going on, how did anyone get anything worthwhile done."

Leaning his head against the cupboard, Dylan closed his eyes. "Ya, we still had plenty of time to train and learn how to fight. It was just the way it was; people could have sex with who they wanted. It was just how our life was."

Callista picked up her plate, then walked around to the sink area. She collected Dylan's plate, having to lean around him in the compact space to get his dishes. She busied herself by rinsing and drying up the ware, and yet she could not keep a grasp on her curiosity.

"Why divulge any of this to me?"

"Why not?"

Callista rolled her eyes, annoyance surging in her. "Are you always this vexing?"

The sound of his laughter slid across her skin like a caress and it took all of her self-control not to shiver, the hairs on the back of her neck rising. Callista dried her hands, angling her body to look at the vampire, and found him looking back at her.

"If you ask my siblings, they will tell you that I am a hundred percent vexing all the time. My mother would tell you that I could find trouble in an empty field. So, I guess the answer to your question is, probably, but you'll have to ask someone else because I think they are all full of shit and I'm like, totally awesome."

Callista wanted to laugh, wanted to just undo the tight hold on her emotions for a little sliver of time and feel what it would be like to be amused. She felt it, simmering in the pit of her stomach, plucking at the fragile threads that held her together. Her stomach threatened to purge the meal she had just eaten, pain ripping through her abdomen, and Callista had to brace her hands on the sink to stop the tremble in her legs.

She truly was unravelling.

When a hand landed on her shoulder, Callista flinched, spinning toward the vampire, and he grasped her wrists, the gentle touch of his fingers around her wrists almost too much for her to take. She realized she was breathing a little too hard for someone who was not affected by emotions, defiantly lifting her gaze to Dylan, the concern in his eyes making her snap out of her current state and erect her walls once again.

"I thought harpies were immortal?"

Callista blinked her eyes, confused, tilting her head to the side as she wondered why he was asking that when it was obvious that something had happened to her a few moments ago. She tracked Dylan's line of sight, then realized that the vampire was staring at her scars.

When she tried to snatch her hands away, the vampire's grip tightened, and while Callista could have easily broken the hold, she simply chose not to.

"I didn't see these when I fed from you?"

"I did not have the sleeves of my tunic rolled up enough for you to see. That is all."

Dylan stepped closer to her, his eyes bleeding to red for a

flash before returning to their normal shade. "Who. Hurt. You?"

This time, Callista did yank her hands back, the imprints of Dylan's grasp on her skin for a moment before they began to fade. "It is part of the training process for harpies. We must learn to not feel the pain, to assimilate it. Harpies may not have feelings, but our brains still understand that a sword in the gut is supposed to hurt. We must learn to not allow that to happen."

Dylan frowned, like he was not happy with her answer. "These marks are a funny shape."

Callista summoned her talons and using her right hand, she pressed the claws against the white scars, careful not to spill any blood.

"They dug their talons into your skin! How fucking old were you?"

Callista rolled down her sleeves, moving away from the close proximity of the vampire and the hurricane of emotions that were storming inside of her. "It is not a big thing. It happened centuries ago." Callista peered at Dylan, saw he was still waiting for an answer and something told her he would not let the conversation finish without an answer.

"I was five years old when I got my first marks. It is the same for every harpy born."

Dylan let loose a string of swear words that would make his friend in the wheelchair proud. "A child? They would hurt a child. Sometimes I really wonder what the fuck is wrong with Inferna."

"The world is full of good and evil people who are just good or evil for no particular reason. It matters not whether they are Inferna or human. That is how the universe remains balanced."

Callista was more than happy to change the topic of conversation, returning to the couch, and lowering herself to it. "How do you propose we get inside your home without detection?"

Dylan strode to where she was sitting, slumped down beside her, before reaching into a secret storage console to his left and withdrawing a mobile phone device. She must have been staring at the device because Dylan informed her that it was an untraceable phone.

"I made sure that no one would know it was me. I only use it to call a certain few people, and it doesn't have the ability to receive incoming calls. I'm not trying to trick you but I do actually have a plan; it will just take some navigating at short notice."

Callista had little choice but to sit back and listen as Dylan called a number, putting it on loudspeaker so that Callista could hear the entire conversation. She wasn't sure if this was the vampire's attempt to get her to trust him, or to lull her into a false sense of security.

"Yeah?"

"JP, it's Mac. Can you talk?"

Callista heard movement, then this JP didn't say anything for a few minutes. There came a sound of a locking door, then the man's voice came back on the line. "Sorry, Mac. What you got for me?"

"I need your discretion and your skills. Can you do me a solid tomorrow night and show up to Club Zero as me and make a scene."

Callista wasn't sure how this JP was going to be able to cast such an illusion that he was Dylan, but it even got stranger. "Can you get Molly on board too? If you take this on, I'll send a photo of who I need her to be. Name your price."

JP whistled down the phone. "Christ, Mac. It must be bad if you are asking me to do this, knowing full well that your family has been all over the asses of every goddamn Inferna looking for you and the succubus. Are you in trouble, mate?"

Dylan leaned back in the seat, his shoulder brushing against Callista and she fought the urge to jerk away from the ghost of his touch. He rested his free hand on the planes of his stomach. "No more than usual, JP. I need something flashy, something that will make sure the full weight of Sicarius comes down on the gaff, then when Jazz shows up, just give her the safe word and she will know you and Molly are working for me."

A hearty chuckle came down the line. "The last time I did that Jasmine almost ripped me limb from limb. Only you and her would use pineapple as a fucking code word."

Callista watched as Dylan's lips curved into a smile that seemed sad, a contemplative look on his face. "This is time-sensitive, JP. Are you in?"

"You know I am. Molly too. You know she can't say no to your handsome face."

Jealousy rippled through Callista, unwanted and uncon-trollable. Her talons unleashed, ripping into the fabric of the couch with an audible ripping sound, and Callista snapped her gaze up to see Dylan looking at her with a bemused expression on his face.

CHAPTER EIGHT

Dylan

It was subtle, the tiny pinprick of emotion that Dylan was able to ascertain from Callista, like it was something his magic was picking up at a great distance. Her physical reaction was more obvious. It was as if she had heard JP's comment and was angered by the fact that another woman would be interested in him.

Interesting.

Dylan hadn't spent that much time with the harpy, but there was no denying she was hiding secrets, maybe even trying to conceal secrets from Dante as well. Could Dylan get her to trust him enough to reveal what she was keeping to herself? And could he then in turn betray that trust to ensure his family was safe?

Mine.

Dylan tried to push the possessive thought from his mind as he heard JP chuckle down the phone, but Dylan focused only on Callista as he answered. "Molly has about as much interest in me as you do, mate. Isn't she still with her most recent girlfriend?"

"Nah, mate. That ended months ago. She's part of a throuple now."

Dylan snorted, running his hands through his hair as he watched a horrified Callista surge to her feet and stalk to the window as he concluded his call with JP, promising to send over the photos Molly would need to become Callista.

The harpy was staring out the window, her arms wrapped around her waist as if she were afraid that she might lose control again. Dylan approached Callista cautiously, holding up the phone. "I need to take your picture for Molly."

Callista angled her body toward Dylan, that blank expression firmly back on her face. "Why?"

"JP and Molly are brother and sister. They have the ability to change shape into any person they have seen a photo of or seen in person. I've had JP pretend to be me on a few occasions when I needed a little peace and quiet."

Tilting her head in a way that Dylan was starting to notice the harpy did when she was about to ask a question, Callista asked. "Do you need peace and quiet a lot?"

"More than I care to admit."

The only response Dylan got was a slight incline of Callista's head. Then she turned to face him, the full brunt of her stare held his, and if Dylan still required air to breathe, then she would have stolen it away from him. Bright green eyes that were so otherworldly in colour, Dylan wanted to tilt her chin upward so he could study the angles of her face.

Her features were striking, a sharpness in her cheekbones that elongated her jaw and chin. Her blue hair hung in a tangle around her shoulders, and Dylan wanted so badly to fist his hand in her hair and pull her forward for a kiss to see if that would satisfy the hunger in him, or whether it would further ignite the flames in his veins.

Instead, Dylan reached out and tucked a strand of hair behind Callista's ears, saw the pointed tips, and realized that she must have dropped the illusion so that Dylan could get an accurate picture.

"Explain to me your plan."

The timber of her tone had dropped, but it was still clipped. Dylan kept his own face unreadable as he traced a finger down her jawline, hoping to draw out another flare of emotion.

Unfortunately, Callista's walls were firmly back in place.

"The plan is," Dylan began, holding up his phone to snap a picture. "JP will go to one of my fave clubs, act like me for a couple of hours, with someone bound to send word to my family. Then Molly will show up as you, and we will fight and cause a scene. Malakai will ensure that Sicarius arrive in great numbers because you are dangerous, and it will distract them all enough for us to slip undetected into my own goddamn house without alerting attention."

Callista raised an eyebrow. "From what I know of your brother, he is a smart vampire. Do you really think he will fall for that and clear out the entire building and leave it undefended?"

Well, when she put it like that it made him feel like a stupid idiot.

"My brother is smart. He would realize that if I somehow managed to escape, then I'd be hungry so would go feed, before I came back to Sicarius. Unless you have any other ideas, Blue? I'm all ears."

Dylan gently gripped Callista's chin, turning her face so that he could snap another picture and then he felt Callista's breath on his fingers as she replied.

"Malakai would never believe that you would go party when your family is in danger. The bond you all share, mates included, is far too entwined to even consider that you would not rather starve than leave Scarlett alone with Vindicta for more time than necessary. What needs to happen is the later part of your plan. JP will go to Dante's and then Molly will come in and they can fight, like I am trying to recapture you."

Dylan couldn't help but look at the harpy, realizing her mind was as sharp as her talons and it did nothing to dampen his awareness of her. His gums ached as his fangs threatened to elongate. Unable to stop himself, Dylan leaned in and grazed his nose just under her jaw, at the curve of her neck.

Jesus, she smelled like frost on grass after a winter's night.

He wanted to have another taste of her, wanted to sink his fangs into her neck while inside her, those wicked talons of hers digging into his flesh. Dylan shuddered, a low rumble in his chest.

He intended to close the minuscule distance between them, and it was then he felt the burn of gold against his flesh, scented the charring, welcomed the blissful agony at his stomach before he stepped back, holding up his hands as he glanced down, spotted the solid gold dagger still pointed at his stomach, as well as the raging hard-on that tented his lounge pants.

The harpy was trying very hard not to glance downward.

"Hey, I'm sorry. I got carried away. Blame it on being an empath."

"I do not care. I have no feelings. However, too many people take what they want from me. You do not get to take what you want from me. I am not a slave to you."

Dylan opened his mouth to answer, heard the fierceness in her tone, and was even more ashamed of his behaviour after hearing what Callista had to say. He kept his hands up, knowing saying sorry again would be futile so he stood there, the tip of the gold dagger against his skin until Callista flicked her hand and the dagger was whipped from his skin and sheathed at her waist.

Most Inferna were not aware of all vampires most guarded secret, but obviously, Dante had filled Callista in on it. Silver wouldn't kill a vampire; that was just a rumour that TV and movies had heightened. It was actually gold that was the weapon of choice if you wanted to kill a vampire. Or decapitation, although, Dylan had heard stories of a really old vampire who had survived even that.

Dante had sent them a golden stake back when Malakai and Keeva first got together, a centuries-old tradition when one Kiss wanted to advise of a grievance against another. It was a show that they were willing to go to permanent death in order to have themselves heard.

His body was screaming at him to have another taste of Callista, to sink his fangs into skin only he had drunk from. To strip her bare and fuck her on the floor while he tasted her.

Mate.

Mate.

Mate.

Dylan stepped back as his fangs elongated, turning his back to Callista so that he could regain his composure. He went to the fridge, took two bottles of blood from it, then proceeded to drain both bottles while Callista watched him with a guarded expression.

Jesus, was this how Malakai and Zeke had felt near their mates? Hell, he had drunk three bottles of blood and he was still hungry for a taste of her. How the fuck had Zeke managed to survive on that crap for so many years? The bloodlust that stirred inside him felt as if he was trying to swallow the emotions of the ripper vampire once more.

For years, Dylan had siphoned the anger, resentment and hunger that ate at Zeke, taking those emotions upon himself so much that he almost broke. Dealing with your own emotions was hard enough, trying to conquer someone else's had made him suicidal.

It made him think about the worst time, hell, the very worst of times, when had it not been for Malakai, he would have killed himself.

Dylan couldn't tell where he ended and Zeke's emotions began. It was one and the same, at this stage, a never-ending wave of self-hatred that had Dylan craving oblivion. He was supposed to be finalizing security plans for their new home, right in the heart of Cork City. Instead, he was having a full fucking mental breakdown in the middle of what would become the family's main living area.

Jasmine had been helping him, but Dylan had sent her away hours ago, to look after the planning for the bar they intended to open, alongside their security company as the legitimate side of their business, so he had spent most of the night by himself.

Earlier in the evening, Malakai had brought a vile human rapist to the house they were staying in while the new building was being completed. Zeke had been crazed with bloodlust, the scene like something from a horror movie as the other vampire ripped the human apart, not caring that his heart no longer beat after he snapped his neck because while dead, he still had blood in him.

After, when the haze of bloodlust had cleared, Zeke had looked at the mangled body, looked at the blood staining his hands and clothing, and the wave of emotions had hit Dylan like a freight train.

Anger, repulsion, self-hatred, guilt and fear; Dylan had to endure it all because even with the walls he had erected inside himself, the strength of Zeke's emotions was so raw, so powerful, that Dylan's magic wanted a taste of it. Of its own accord, the magic brushed against the storm of feelings, and before Dylan was ready, it swallowed it all down, burying it in what felt like the epicentre of Dylan's chest, and he had to sit down and rest his head in his hands so that no one would see the tears in his eyes.

His magic turned Zeke's feelings inward, forcing Dylan to feel repulsed at himself, to hate himself, and what he was. And he was so angry that he hadn't been strong enough to stop being changed into a vampire, that he was now condemned to a life as a monster, a creature of darkness with no soul, and no chance for redemption.

Zeke hadn't even cared that Dylan was hurting, he just stormed off, leaving Malakai to call a cleaning crew, and Jasmine to come and run her fingers through his hair, trying to soothe him.

She thinks you're weak. Your own sister thinks that you are weak.

Dylan lifted his hands from his face to see Malakai looking right at him, a frown on his face. He could feel the worry emulating from Malakai and the sadness rolling off of Jasmine and it made Dylan's chest want to explode.

Surging from the chair, Dylan had declared that he was going to go work on the plans for the building. Kai had sent Jazz with him to *keep an eye on him and he had been almost grateful when a problem arose at the club that Jasmine had to go handle.*

No more work had been done since Jasmine had left, Dylan slumping down to the floor, sitting by the window with his knees to his chest, the weight of the emotions crippling him as he let loose the cascade of tears that had been fucking building behind his eyes for hours.

Opening his mouth, he unleashed a pained scream, his fingers going to his hair and Dylan yanked hard, pulling clumps of it out until he scented blood. Releasing his hair, Dylan clenched a fist and punched the concrete floor, splintering both the floor and his hand at the same time. The pain rippled from his fingers to his knuckles and up his arm and jolting Dylan from the swell of Zeke's emotions.

For fuck sake, he was pitiful. A burden to his family. He couldn't even stand to look at himself in the mirror, how could they even claim to love him?

Dylan felt the bones in his hand start to fix themselves and he hated it. He wanted to feel the pain. He wanted to know that this was real and he was living this life. The women and men he took to bed made him feel alive for only a couple of hours and then when he felt like his heart was beating so hard in his chest, he realized it was not his own heart, and merely him hearing and feeling his partners' heart racing.

He had long since stopped allowing blood to pump to his heart, the beating feeling so hollow that he could not control the unbearable sadness when his heart did manage to beat from a massive intake of blood.

It reminded him that he was undead…

Dylan had planned to import bulletproof, sun-repellent glass but it hadn't arrived just yet, and Dylan felt the sun begin to rise in the distance. If he sat here, just sat here for another while, then the sun would do what his mind had been screaming at him to do for years. The sun would singe his skin, set it alight, and consume him until he was nothing more than ashes on the concrete floor.

Malakai and Jasmine would mourn him, and yet, he knew they would be better off without him. Zeke would probably have to die as well without Dylan to swallow his emotions, but just like with Dylan's death, it would lessen the burden for them.

Isolde would finish the build. She had worked with him to finalize everything.

It really would be for the best.

Dylan closed his eyes, feeling the first blissful burn of agony as the sun's rays glided along his skin. He was old enough that it would take time, his death, and it would hurt. And yet, the pain would be his own, he would die as himself, and it was worth all the agony that was coming.

He had never felt such peace.

The smell of burnt flesh hit him and he struggled to keep his eyes closed, fought against his body's need to flee out of the sun's grasp and stop the torment. He was concentrating so hard on stopping his instincts that he never heard the elevator door open or sensed anyone coming into the room.

"Dylan!"

He heard his name being roared from Malakai's lips, then he was dragged out of the harmful rays of the sun, and Dylan lunged for Malakai, angry that his brother had snatched his chance at peace away. But Malakai was stronger than he was, holding Dylan to him, hugging him as Dylan sobbed and screamed because Malakai had stopped him from dying.

Dylan opened his eyes to look at Callista, the harpy having just finished braiding her hair, her eyes looking out as dawn began to arrive. Her sword was lying across her lap and as if she sensed his eyes on her, Callista peered over her shoulder for a moment, those almost lime-green eyes roaming his body with no expression at all before she returned to her current task.

"If we are to be stuck here for the day, then perhaps we should rest. As you said before, you have not had much sleep."

"That sounds like you want to get me into bed, Blue." Dylan teased, earning a snort from the harpy.

"If it only means I would get some peace. I did not know vampires liked to talk so much."

Dylan chuckled, walking over to the couch and sitting down beside her, pretending not to notice when Callista moved slightly away from him. She withdrew a cloth from her pocket and started to clean her blade.

"Hey, you can have the bed. I'll sleep out here. Unless you want to snuggle? I kinda feel like you'd be a spooner. Am I right?" Dylan needled her a little more but his words seemed to fall flat.

"I do not sleep. Especially in the homes of vampires I do not trust. Should anyone dare come through the door to try and aid you, I will kill them. Do not sleep away the entire day, we will leave the moment the sun sets."

Dylan had never felt so thoroughly dismissed in his entire life, and it highly amused him as he bounced to his feet and turned to look at Callista who didn't even bother to lift her gaze from her sword.

"You can come wake me if I sleep too late. And if you're curious, feel free to wake me with your hands wrapped around my cock. I'd wake a happy vampire."

He expected Callista to ignore him, to give him one of her ice-cold glares before returning to her task, but what Dylan wasn't expecting was her to trade barbs with him.

"I could wake you with many hands around your neck, vampire. It would be preferable. My talons might just slice off your cock. I do not know if the appendage would grow back."

Dylan laughed so hard that it startled the harpy, her eyebrows meeting as she glared at him, making him stride toward the bedroom, feeling her eyes on him. Casting a glance over his shoulder, Dylan grinned, winking. "You've watched me long enough, Blue. What makes you think that thinking about you with your talons unsheathed while fisting my cock doesn't turn me on? I didn't realize you were into kink, Blue."

He was still busting a gut laughing as Dylan entered his bedroom, felt the heat in the harpy's eyes as she looked like she wanted to murder him. The saying was true, Dylan was starting to realize; there was a thin line between love and hate...or in his case, lust and hate.

CHAPTER NINE

Callista

CALLISTA WAS ASHAMED AT HERSELF FOR LETTING THE VAMPIRE get under her skin, for letting his crass remarks make her body feel flush and her skin tingly. He had still been laughing as he retired to his room, then like a switch being turned off, she heard not a sound. For a moment, Callista had thought that he might have given her the slip, not considering that he might just be sleeping.

Her unease had prompted her to get to her feet and check, prying open the door, swallowing hard when she realized the vampire had fallen asleep on his stomach, on top of the bed linens, lying sideways on a bed big enough for a whole Kiss of vampires. Her eyes had adjusted to the darkness and landed on the firm curved buttocks that had made lots of insane thoughts rush through Callista's head.

She wholly blamed the vampire for indicating that he would not be opposed to her talons in his skin, but only in a sexual manner. Despite knowing that he was testing her, Callista foolishly wondered if Dylan was actually interested in her in that way. Having watched him so much more than any other Sicarius Security personnel, she knew that he loved to flirt, to tease. He had even spent time teasing the obscurum's mate, the succubus, and it had annoyed Callista.

She looked at her reflection in the glass, and frowned. Her features were nothing special, not in comparison to the women she usually saw Dylan with. If her hair and eyes were not so distinctive, then eyes would skim past her in a room.

Callista shook her head, jerking her face to the right to stop herself from being so idiotic. She wanted to blame the continuing loss of control on the magics that kept her emotions in check for her thinking, but Callista would be fooling herself if she did not admit that even when Vindicta had recharged her mark, she had been fascinated with the vampire.

Safe in the knowledge that the vampire was asleep, Callista took off her long tunic and placed her palm over the symbol etched into her flesh. The bindrune had long since faded, once a vivid black, now a murky shade of grey. Before, when Callista grazed her fingers over the mark, the shock of power emulating from it sent a spark of electricity through her. Now, it barely registered.

Vindicta's plan was nearly at fruition. Callista knew that despite the hundreds of years that she had been by his side, once he achieved what he wanted to achieve, then he may just kill her. It wasn't that Callista wanted to die, but, she would do anything to be free.

It would do her no good if she did not rest for a time, and Callista never truly slept; she was always alert even when asleep, not trusting her environment at all. Laying down on the couch, Callista placed her hands under her head and closed her eyes, but not before she had placed her sword within her reach.

The night had long since fallen on Litochoro, the place where the Greek gods once roamed the mouth of Mount Olympus. Callista had waited until the older members of her Nest had gone off for a night of fornication and fighting, Spartans travelling for miles to bed the infamous harpy warriors in the hopes of breeding a harpy daughter, before she traipsed out of her hut and to the training ground.

Callista had always wondered why the Spartans would risk birthing a child like her, one plagued with human emotions, a warrior who had to train night and day to be as ruthless as the other females in her age group. Her mother had, since her birth, taken precautions so that she would not become pregnant by a Spartan again, not wanting to forgo the rutting, but not wanting to risk another child like Callista.

Not that any bedfellow her mother rutted with would know, for if they failed in their task to impregnate a harpy, the man was deemed not worthy and shunned by all other harpies. Her mother was one of the highest-ranking warriors so her word was believed.

With a sigh, Callista tried to ignore the sounds of swords clanging closer to the tavern and the moans and groans of pleasure, heat rising in her cheeks as she hefted her sword up and practiced her stances. She continued to run her drills until sweat soaked her skin, the light breeze doing nothing to compensate for the stifling heat.

At ten years old, Callista was not even ranked among her class. That fact had been enough just days ago to bring tears to her eyes, her trainer slapping her hard across the face when she did actually cry that it left a welt on her face for the entire day. While her class-mates seemed to just absorb the information, hungry to taste first blood, Callista always felt like she was second-guessing her moves, wondering if she could avoid striking a killing blow, and just wound them.

But there was no honour in wounding her mother told her, only in the death of the enemy.

Callista lifted her sword over her head, slashing downward as she snarled in frustration.

"You are leaving yourself open to attack."

A deep rumble of a voice made Callista spin round, sword held as if bracing for an attack. Before her stood a Spartan, and by his attire, Callista knew he was considered to be an elite soldier. He wore a cloak that reminded Callista of blood and it made her feel a little sick. This Spartan was dressed in the finest breastplate and armour, his leather skirts hanging over muscular thighs.

He had long tresses, like most Spartans, and his dark eyes watched Callista, as he stayed at the fringes of the training field, a smile playing on his lips like she amused him.

"If you attack with your sword held like that, you are likely to lose your guts, little warrior."

The Spartan took a step toward her, coming under the light of the moon and Callista could see that the warrior was handsome, as if he had stepped from Olympus himself, a god among men. She had seen a tapestry of Achilles before, and this soldier, this man, he had the look of Achilles.

"Can I show you?" he asked, coming toward her, and Callista knew if she ran away now, when the Spartan was only offering his aid, her sisters would scoff at her and then she truly would become an outcast.

Her instincts were screaming at her to run away, to find her mother and tell her about the Spartan wandering through their home, a place where they were not permitted. And yet, Callista stood as the soldier reached out his hand, placing his palm on the blade like it would not be able to slice through his flesh and bone, and angled it sideways.

She adjusted her body to be able to strike out with the sword, practiced and the Spartan smiled. "That's it. I suspect the sword is too heavy for you. A girl with such delicate features should wield a lighter weapon."

"It is my sister's blade." Callista heard herself say. "I will not get a blade of my own until I come of age."

That seemed to please the man because his smile widened, Callista tilting her head to the side to get a better look at his face. The soldier took the sword from her hand, setting it down in the sand, then reached out and tucked a strand of hair behind her ear.

"And a harpy does not come of age until they have their first bleeding."

Callista's throat went dry as she nodded, the spartan crouching down in front of her and in his eyes, Callista noticed that the warmth that had been there a moment ago was no longer there.

"How old are you little harpy?"

Something told Callista that she should not answer, that she should kick and scream and get as far away from this soldier as possible, but alas, fear held her immobile. If this was one of her sisters, they would have already unleashed their talons, striking at the soldier for even daring to step into the bounds of their home.

Glancing toward the revelry, Callista sucked in a breath to scream when the soldier grabbed her chin and forced her to look back at him.

"I asked of your age, harpy."

"I...I... I am ten cycles old."

The smile that curved the Spartan's lips was the first evil that Callista had ever seen. She had not realized that humans could be monsters too, as he brushed a thumb over her lips and she wanted to vomit.

"Unclaimed, untouched. I watched you for days, little harpy. So unusual, that hair and those eyes. Not as beautiful as most of your kin, but I could keep you in a cage to see if you bloom. I think it's time you became a woman."

Callista could do nothing but yelp as the soldier grabbed her throat, and swept her legs from under her so that her back hit the sand. The soldier's weight almost crushing her smaller body as tears sprang from her eyes and the soldier chortled, before he leaned in and licked the tears from her cheeks, as if her fear was enjoyable to him.

Now Callista knew about rutting, knew that in order for a woman to become pregnant, a male needed to insert his cock into the woman and that was rutting. It was forbidden within the harpies until two year cycles after a harpy first bled.

The soldier kept her pinned in the sand, hoisting up his skirts and fondling his groin as Callista struggled beneath him. She kicked up on instinct, catching the soldier in his stomach and he stumbled back. Callista tried to scramble back, screaming as loud as she possibly could, knowing that it was unlikely she would be heard over the noise in the village.

"Stupid bitch. Now I'll make it hurt more."

The soldier went to grab for her again and Callista acted on pure instinct. She unsheathed her talons and lashed out, catching the man in the eye, and he let loose a howl of agony, stumbling back. Callista launched herself at him, pushing him down to the sands as he shielded his face.

With a shriek, Callista straddled his chest, striking blindly with her talons, tearing flesh and bone as she lost herself to a blood craze. Blood splattered her skin but she did not care. The solider was pleading now, trying to muster the strength to fight back against his victim, and yet, Callista continued to strike at him.

She vaguely heard the sound of her name; the sound of metal being unsheathed. The man's hands fell away from his face, and Callista could smell his fear as she slashed one last time with her talons, and ripped out the soldier's throat.

Blood gurgled as the soldier's eyes widened, then he went lifeless, the blood still seeping out to stain the sands. Callista scrambled back off the dead soldier's body, tears now flowing unabashed from her eyes as she glanced up to see her mother crouching down in front of her, asking her what had happened.

She was very aware that a number of Spartans had arrived to argue and seek vengeance for the murder of their slain compatriot, but they were held back by the seasoned warriors of her Nest.

"He was trying to rut with me, mother." Her words drew a shocked gasp from the other harpies. "He knew my age and he tried to rut with me. I killed him."

A harpy's first kill was celebrated as it signalled their path to greatness. This would not be celebrated because Callista had killed a man who wanted to take what was not his. The shock hit Callista and she started to tremble as her mother rose and addressed the soldiers.

"This man pissed on the allegiance between harpy and humans. He tried to rape one of our daughters and she defended herself as is her right. Anyone who has issue with this, step forward and take it up with me. Your blood will soon join his."

Not one soldier stepped forward and the crowd dispersed, some of the harpies going to the slain man and taking coin and jewels from his body. Callista's mother dragged her to her feet, supporting her when she nearly collapsed.

"Do not show weakness. Do not give them any more excuses. You did well tonight, Callista."

It was the most praise that her mother had ever bestowed on her, however it did little to soothe her nightmares or help her fit in more with her kin. Less than twelve months later, her mother had sold her to Vindicta.

When she closed her eyes, she saw not the way the soldier had pinned her to the sands, but the havoc she had inflicted on his body and the hot blood that splashed her skin.

Callista bolted away with a shout, her sword clattering to the ground as she held out her hands, gulping in air. For a moment, she could not remember where she was, and it caused panic to flare in her chest. Then cool hands held her face gently, and Callista looked not into dead eyes, but eyes of blue-green that seemed very much alive.

"Hey, deep breaths, okay? Inhale then exhale." Dylan told her, his voice soothing and she complied. "That's it, Callie. That's it, just breathe."

First Blue and now Callie... it was very hard not to like this vampire.

When it seemed like Dylan was about to move his hands from her face, Callista snapped out her hands and gripped his wrists. It was a major lack of control that she would ulti-mately regret, but in this moment, Callista craved the touch. If she was a true harpy, then she would not have had the nightmares.

"I have nightmares too, yano." Dylan told her, his thumb tracing her skin. "Sometimes, they're not even my own."

"And did you see my nightmare?" She asked him, thankful when he shook his head.

"No, I didn't. To be up front and honest, I did try and take away the spike of fear I felt but you blocked my power somehow."

Callista dropped her hold on Dylan's wrist. "It was not my fear you felt. I do not have feelings."

The vampire's lips tugged up at the corners. "Keep telling yourself that, Callie. Won't make it true."

Dylan leaned back on his hunches, his gaze zoning in on the mark etched over her heart and Callista realized she was in a state of undress. "Huh, I would not have expected an Inferna with Greek heritage to get a Norse rune." The vampire reached out to touch the mark, yelped, and stood up straight shaking his hand. "Bloody hell, that hurt. That's some serious mojo for a tattoo."

Callista grabbed her tunic, pulled it on as Dylan went to the kitchen to grab a bottle of blood and as he drank, he poured her a glass of orange juice. She wandered over to the kitchen, watching his throat bob as he drank, aware that Dylan was watching her too.

"So, you wanna tell me what the nightmare was about?"

Time ticked by as Callista mulled over whether or not she should give Dylan the truth, though she felt like it would be of benefit to her to be honest, since it was obvious the vampire suspected she was lying about having feelings. In the grand scheme of things, Callista had little to lose at this point.

"I dreamt of the night I first killed a man." Callista explained, taking a drink before she continued. "I was practicing my sword work when he trespassed and then tried to rut with me. I ripped out his throat. It was young for a harpy to have a first kill. It was not long after my mother sold me to Dante."

"How old were you?"

The vampire's tone had dropped to a dangerous level, leaving Callista to roll her eyes, pretending the fact that Dylan sounding protective, didn't send a rush of warmth coursing through her.

"I was ten when I killed the Spartan and eleven when my mother sold me. And before you growl and puff your chest, it was a long time ago and I am alive and the Spartan is dead. It is inconsequential."

Dylan set his bottle down on the counter and licked his lips, Callista's eyes watching the subtle movement, before he spoke. "First of all, I don't puff my chest. Second of all, I would have given anything to see you rip out the asshole's throat. Tiny fierce Callie."

Sighing as she rolled her eyes, Callista went to finish getting dressed when Dylan stopped her by calling her name. She angled her body towards him as he came over to her, pointed at her clothing.

"We need to go incognito. You can't wear your own clothing because we need to stay under the radar."

Tilting her head, Callista noted the mischief that danced in Dylan's eyes as she replied. "I did not bring any alternative clothing with me. That is all I have to wear."

The vampire stepped closer to her, placing a hand on the small of her back, the contact searing as the magics in her mark slipped even further, Callista struggling to keep her composure as Dylan leaned in and whispered in her ear. "I got you covered, Blue. I have the perfect sneaking clothes for you." He led her to the bedroom, then turned to her with a smile that made Callista's heart race. "Let's get you naked."

Callista suppressed a shudder, the vampire having no clue just how tempting his words were.

CHAPTER TEN

Callista

CALLISTA HAD MANAGED TO REIN IN THE SUDDEN URGES THAT had her core tightening and her breasts aching as the vampire handed her clothing that was obviously Sicarius issued. Then she had been surprised when Dylan had simply stripped off in front of her, yanking down his lounge pants to reveal his uncovered rear-end. Callista had stood there, gaping at him up until the moment he went to turn around.

It was then Callista fled to the bathroom with a feeble excuse that she needed to freshen up. Even through the locked door she could hear his laughter and instead of annoying her, it made Callista want to smile with him.

Oh, this was bad…very bad indeed.

Callista stripped off her tunic and pants, frowning for a moment before she removed her undergarments and then dressed in the clothing Dylan had provided her. First, she slipped on the shorts styled panties, and the sports bra, trying not to think of how he knew her sizing or how he had been able to acquire them so quickly when no one had delivered anything.

The black skin-tight leggings seemed to mould to her skin, more flexible than they looked, and then she yanked the vest over her head, the material the same as the leggings, but they were fashioned so that Callista could move and fight in them.

Turning to look at herself in the mirror, Callista pulled her blue hair off her face and rebraided it, so that it would not impede her if she had to fight. When she felt that she was suitably dressed, Callista opened the bathroom door, stepping outside to find Dylan perched at the end of his bed waiting for her.

His mouth slightly parted, his eyes devouring her like he wanted to take a bite out of her, and perhaps he did. Callista deposited her clothing on a chair just outside the bathroom, suddenly self-conscious about her less than sultry body.

Not that you could tell from the way the vampire was looking at her.

Dylan whistled through his teeth. "Damn, Blue. That looks almost sinful on you. Who the hell knew you were hiding that body under those frumpy clothes?"

"My clothing is not frumpy." She argued, but compared to what she was wearing now, Callista knew they were.

Dylan rose to his feet, this time, it was Callista who found herself devouring him with her eyes. He wore black utility pants and a plain black tee that clung to his muscular frame. His long blond strands had been pulled into a knot on top of his head, and Callista frowned as she took an involuntary step toward him, causing the corners of his mouth to kick up.

"Keep looking at me like that, Blue, and I might just give in to the never-ending urge I have to taste your lips."

Callista did not lower her gaze, feeling emboldened, madness surely taking hold of her and all common sense fleeing. The vampire moved in a blur, then her back was hitting the wall with an oomph, and Dylan's lips were at her throat and a long, almost pained moan slipped free of her lips.

Her palms slapped against the wall, because even in the midst of losing her mind, Callista knew if she touched Dylan, then she would give in and let him rut with her.

"I wish we had more time. I wish I could take my time with you." Dylan muttered against her neck.

Callista's breath caught in her throat as the vampire grazed his fangs over the pulse. But instead of biting her, he closed his mouth over her pulse and sucked hard, no doubt it would leave a mark but the thought of it did not bother Callista as much as she thought it would.

Resting his forehead against her own, Dylan barked out a curse before he retreated, the fog of lust clearing and Callista cursed herself for her lapse in judgement. She pushed away from the wall as the vampire came forward with a black zip hoodie, holding it out when Callista went to take it from him, leaving her with no choice but to allow him to slip her arms through it.

When it was on, he turned her back around and zipped the hoodie all the way up, mumbling that it was a shame to hide her perfect handfuls of breasts away. She might have laughed at him then, had he not tilted her chin, gently pressing his lips to hers for a fleeting second before he stepped back, leaving Callista dumbfounded.

"You and I," Dylan began as he zipped up his own hoodie after donning it, "Will finish that kiss later. I promise you."

Callista rolled her eyes, striding from the bedroom to put some distance between them and douse the flames that seemed to have ignited in her veins. She should have left him on the road the night she had taken Scarlett. It would have been easier to do so...and yet, Callista had not been able to fight the compulsion telling her that she had to take him too.

Concentrating on the task at hand, Callista managed to finesse her sheath to make allowances for her outfit, not feeling comfortable leaving it here even though she shouldn't need it. When her mother sold her, Callista had been somewhat skilled, but it did not slip her memory that the vampire who purchased her had trained her to be the warrior she was now.

Long ago, he had laughed with her. There had been times when he was not consumed with his vengeance and though he was not her parent, Dante had been more of a parental figure than her own mother. But then the laughter dwindled, the moments when Dante was the man who had laughed with her vanished, as Vindicta smothered those emotions, Dante became eclipsed.

"You sorted?"

Callista lifted her head, marvelling at how easily Dylan had adjusted to the times, his Irish accent, more his Cork accent even, like he was not centuries old and from a different time. She inclined her head, following after him as he exited the apartment and headed back down to the tunnels below. He descended the ladder first, then stood and watched as she climbed down, reaching for her hips to help her down off the last rung, setting her on her feet.

"Which way, Blue?"

Callista didn't respond verbally to his question, simply strode back down the darkened tunnel. It surprised her that it had only taken hours for the tension she had felt on their felt journey through the tunnels to all but evaporate. It wasn't that she trusted the vampire not to betray her if his family asked it of him, no she expected it and would think less of him if he gave away his loyalty because he was intrigued by her. Yet she knew that he would not hurt her like many had before.

They traipsed through the damp dark tunnels in relative silence, the only sound was the cheerful whistling that Dylan did, low enough that only she could hear him. He liked music, the vampire, she knew that from watching him, and from watching the seer. They loved to party and drink and dance.

One night, when watching them, she had observed a conversation between the wolf and the banshee, the wolf almost panting after the seer, and the banshee, she was merely amused by the crowd that was watching the brother and sister with lustful expressions.

"We should charge people just to come watch the wonder twins dance."

The wolf chuckled at the banshee, his eyes never leaving the seer, his eyes tinged with amber. "It's insane, Keeva. Every goddamn night. All I'm waiting for is for Fabio to let loose his blondie locks and those humans might just orgasm right there."

Keeva, the banshee barked out a laugh. "Jesus, Fabio... that's gonna stick now."

"You need to ask your fiancé if their father was part siren or some shit. It's the only reason I can think of why so many of the saps look like they would gladly toss themselves into the ocean to dance with them."

The banshee elbowed the wolf in human skin. "Does that include you, Roman? There's some drool on your chin."

The wolf shoved the banshee and they laughed, but even Callista had lingered in the shadows transfixed by the sensual dancing and when the empath had looked toward where she was hidden in the shadows, Callista had almost broken cover to go to him.

"What was your father?"

"What?" Dylan asked, confused by her sudden question.

Callista kept walking forward, trying to think how to rephrase her question. "I am a harpy because my mother was one. I overheard the wolf and the banshee talking about you and your sister and they wondered if your father had some siren in him. I observed you both, alone and together, and I often wondered that myself. Since you were an empath before you became a vampire, and your sister was a seer, it makes sense that some of your parentage was Inferna."

They veered off down toward the exit to the building across from Sicarius, the path widening so Dylan fell into step beside her. They walked a little, side by side, not speaking, their shoulders almost touching.

"We've often wondered that ourselves but by the time we were old enough to ask those questions, our village was attacked by vampires, and only me, Kai, Dante, and Jazz survived. Malakai tried to do all this genetic testing but we never managed to narrow it down. Guess we'll just have to remain enigmas to the world."

Callista snorted, glaring at him in the dark. "You sound almost pleased with that."

"I am. If you weren't so intrigued by me, I'd have no chance getting you naked."

"You already do not have any chance, vampire."

The vampire in question grinned. "I hope you're not a gambler, Blue, because your poker face sucks. You just haven't admitted it to yourself yet. You will."

Suppressing a snarl of frustration, Callista stopped at a doorway, pushing it open and headed up the winding stairs that would bring them to the rooftop. The wind whipped against her skin the moment she emerged to stand on the roof, a raindrop hitting her nose as she lifted her face to the sky for a moment and breathed in the night air.

Awareness prickled her skin, and Callista turned to face Dylan, the vampire watching her with amusement. She felt she needed to explain, just intending to give Dylan a little knowledge but ended up divulging more about herself than she should.

"I had never seen rain, real rain, until after Dante purchased me. I was so shocked at its wetness, at its hardness that anytime it rained, I wanted to dance under it. It was silly, as a child, experiencing the seasons. I almost fainted the first time Dante showed me snow."

"Maybe some day I can show you my favourite place to snowboard."

He sounded so earnest, like he truly wanted to show her this place that meant something to him and yet, in another life perhaps, it would have meant a lot to her that he would show her. However, their lives were complicated and bloody and messy and Callista did not like mess.

Talons ripping flesh, blood coating her hands.

Clamping her lips shut, Callista walked to the edge of

the building and narrowed her gaze. She had spent count-less hours here, watching the comings and goings, studying the shift patterns. She knew the employees with the least access and the most access. She had been standing on the ledge when Sniper had fired the shot at Malakai Cavanagh and his aim would have hit true had his banshee not saved him.

It was on this very roof that Callista had aimed an arrow at Dylan, pulling up at the last minute because she found she could not aim for his heart. And then she had lied to Vindicta and told him that Dylan had heard the arrow and moved at the last moment, meaning she hit his shoulder and not his heart.

It was Vindicta's own hubris that he had believed her lies.

"Okay," Dylan said, striding up to her, folding his arms across his chest after glancing at his watch, one Callista hadn't even seen him put on. "JP should be starting to get noticed now and the building will empty out. Once we see them leave, we can get in using a side door that no one has access to but me. I'll need you to stay quiet while I override the system."

Callista inclined her head, showing him that she under-stood, just as a flurry of activity started across the river. Malakai Cavanagh strode out barking orders and black armoured SUVs screeched to a halt in front of the building, blocking the Primus from view.

"We should make tracks." Dylan said, drawing her atten-tion from the building to the vampire, before she shifted her gaze back to see the werewolf punching in a code that sealed the building shut before he jogged over to the last remaining SUV and jumped into the passenger seat.

Dylan was already heading down the fire escape at the side of the building, leaving Callista with no choice but to follow him. They stuck to the shadows, the smiling, teasing expression all but vanished from the vampire's face as he led her not to the main door of the Sicarius building, but to the underground carpark.

Back against the cold concrete, Callista saw the hesitation in Dylan's movements, saw the conflict in his eyes. Dylan walked her to the farthest point of the carpark, frowning when it appeared that he had simply dragged her to a dead end. He braced his hands on the wall, dropping his head and letting loose a frustrated breath

"We should get on with it. The chameleon won't be able to fool your family for long."

"Forgive me for taking a fucking minute before I betray my entire family. This isn't easy for me."

Reaching out, hoping to offer him some comfort, Callista rested her palm on his arm, his gaze snapping to hers. "I did not think it would be easy for you. You do this so Scarlett has a chance of getting out unscathed. Your family will understand. Besides, they will most certainly focus all their rage and anger on me, they might not even notice you."

Dylan blinked and barked out a laugh, straightening. "Was that a joke, Blue?"

Callista rolled her eyes, swallowing as she said. "Hardly. I was merely stating facts. Your family is out for my blood. If you found that funny, so be it."

Dylan stared at her for a moment, then he let loose a pained growl. He surged forward and Callista thought they were under attack, however that was not the case. He took her face in his hands and kissed her lips, the contact searing her from the inside out, and then she was kissing him back, her hands gripping his hoodie.

The vampire nipped at her lips, causing Callista to gasp, opening her mouth so that Dylan could thrust his tongue into her mouth and Callista followed his lead, letting him set the pace, let him take control of her mouth, licking and sucking until she struggled to breathe.

Dylan pulled his lips from hers with an audible smack and

Callista gulped in air, leaning her head against Dylan's chest so he would not see the emotions that had slipped free of the chains she had leashed them on.

"I won't let anyone hurt you, Blue. I won't let anyone hurt you."

Even you?

That was the question that she wanted to ask of him, because his family might be baying for her blood, but this vampire, this man, he was the one who had her at war with her heart, and Callista feared it was a battle that she just might lose.

She flattened her palms against his chest and gently pushed him away, putting some much-needed distance between them, lifting her gaze defiantly to hold eyes tinged with red.

"We must forge ahead, Dylan. All we can do now is keep going."

It was the first time she had addressed him by his name, and it hit him like a punch as she watched him fight an internal battle with himself, the one where loyalty to his family outweighed whatever was happening between them. She had no such loyalty, no such family who would question her actions or be concerned for her wellbeing.

From the pained expression on Dylan's face, Callista knew she was better off.

Dylan grunted, closing his eyes for a moment as he said. "I wish things were different, Blue. I really fucking do."

Callista waited until Dylan opened his eyes, peering at her, piercing her soul as she replied with as much truth as possible. "As do I. As do I."

The vampire dragged his gaze from Callista's, his palm on the wall like he was caressing it, then she heard a click, watched as a panel came out of the wall and Dylan keyed in a code, the wall rumbling as part of it slid to the side, revealing a secret entrance.

"Remember what I said, Blue. The moment the door closes and we are inside, don't say a word so I can disable the system and make sure not to alert anyone monitoring things. I know you don't trust easily, but if you don't trust me, it's game over. Okay?"

Callista nodded her head, waiting as Dylan went to go inside, then paused, holding out his hand and for a moment. Callista did not understand what it was that he intended for her to do, then she recalled Malakai and Keeva holding hands, Scarlett and the obscurum doing the same.

Slipping her hand into the vampire's felt like the most natural thing in the world. His smile felt like the Greek sunshine on her skin as he curled his fingers into hers and Callista could do nothing but follow him into the dark.

CHAPTER ELEVEN

Dylan

NEVER HAD DYLAN FELT SO AT WAR WITH HIMSELF AS HE DID after indulging in a moment of sheer madness, kissing Callista just before breaking into his home to steal really powerful and old scrolls for his no- so- dead brother. The world had faded away, especially when she kissed him back with a passion that shouldn't be possible.

His mind had been screaming at him for days, intensified now that Callista was his. Would the universe be so cruel as to give him who he had been searching for his entire life but have it so his family would never accept her?

Ya, karma really was a bitch...

Even now, with Callista's fingers entwined in his, Dylan felt more himself than he had in a long time, maybe ever. If push came to shove, Dylan wasn't sure that he would have the strength to walk away from her.

He was fucked either way.

Dylan squeezed Callista's hand as he led her up the stone steps and pushed open the panel leading to his control room. The walls were lined with servers that manned the security on various Sicarius contracts, and then there were more servers freestanding around the room. He knew each port, each server, and which contract it was linked to. It would be his ass if any of them failed so he had made it his business to be involved and learn. He had hired in the brainiest and most qualified computer analysts he could find, eager to learn from them.

Dylan stepped into the room and immediately spoke, knowing that alarms would go off if a certain command was not said within sixty seconds.

"Sicarius, initiate stealth mode 45."

"Stealth Mode 45 initiated, Dylan. Command 23 asking for override."

Shit Isolde had rigged his personal codes.

"Denied, Sicarius. Initiate system loop on all cameras from block 7 to homebase 0, including the library."

There was a tense pause before the AI answered him. "Command 23 already issued a request for an alert should anyone try and breach standard protocol. Permission to advise Command 23 that an override of the security process has taken place?"

"Denied, Sicarius. Please refrain from alerting Command 23 that standard protocol has been overridden. Maintain current status while following my commands and only my commands for the next two hours. I will advise when to resume normal duties."

"Understood, sir. Security cameras have been looped on the direct path to homebase 0."

Dylan thanked the AI, then glanced at Callista who was watching him with wide eyes. She opened her mouth to speak, then clamped it shut as if she remembered Dylan had told her not to speak.

"It's okay, we're good."

Reluctantly letting go of her hand, Dylan went over to his computer desk in this room and opened a drawer, withdrawing a Glock 19 and loading it, then tucked it into one of the loops at his waist. Callista watched him, tense, and he wished she could tell by now that he wasn't about to shoot her.

The same couldn't be said if his family got to her before he could explain.

"How do you kill a harpy?"

"With great difficulty and lots of bloodshed." Came her tart reply and it made Dylan grin. How the fuck did Dante not realize that Callista had been hiding her true self for centuries? Or did he know exactly what she was, a harpy with feelings, and used it to exploit her? That sounded more like something his asshole brother would do.

"I'm not planning on killing you, Blue. I just wanted to know so I can spot a weapon if my family does turn up. I want to protect you."

Callista glared at him, the heat they had shared only minutes ago seemingly forgotten. "I can protect myself. We need to get going. We have wasted enough time already."

Storming to the only door Callista could see, she yanked it open, rushing outside without even checking to see if anyone was lurking in the halls and Dylan quickly followed after her. Her shoulders were tense, her body rigid as Callista paused at the end of the corridor.

They had reached the main lobby of the building, one that had glass windows, and they would have to make a dash across the foyer in case Malakai or Isolde had set a patrol around the building by guards in civies. Dylan couldn't help but glance at the entrance where Callista had shot him, and it caused his lips to curve into a smile.

"What?" Callista asked as Dylan took her hand back in his and lifted her knuckles to his lips.

"That's where we first met...well...kinda...that's where you shot me."

Callista narrowed her gaze, checking to see if he was being serious and when she realized he was, she rolled her eyes. "You are not all the way sane."

"And you think that's kinda hot, right?"

Callista sighed and Dylan winked at her, then tugged her

hand and bolted, using his vampire speed to cross the room and Callista stayed right there with him. Dylan pressed the elevator, waited until it opened, then ducked inside with Callista.

The moment the doors closed, Dylan whirled round, crashing his mouth against Callista's, walking so that her back was to the wall of the elevator. Her hands gripped his upper arms as Dylan trailed his lips down her jaw, to her neck that he had marked before. He needed to mark her again, to claim her, so that anyone who dared harm her would know that she was his.

But she wasn't really his now, was she?

A growl rumbled in his throat as he sucked the spot, and Callista dug her nails, no her talons into his arms, not piercing the skin, but enough to leave a mark of her own.

The elevator opened and Callista pulled back, her lips red from kissing and her pale skin flushed. The kiss had shaken her enough for the glamour on her ears to disappear, the pointed tips protruding out from her hair.

"You must stop doing that." She said, her chest heaving as she tried to get her breath back.

"Kissing you? Why?"

Dylan was eager to know her answer, eager to delve deeper into knowing her, because even if it was madness, even if his family thought him utterly insane, the harpy had wormed her way into his heart. He wanted time to find out all about her...and yet, he knew time wasn't on their side, a point punctuated by Callista in her reply.

"I do not wish for it to pain you if your family kill me. I do not wish for it to hurt if it is you that must kill me."

"Callie..."

Callista stepped off the elevator and into the family room. It looked exactly the same as it had when he had left, from the blanket that Scarlett like to pull over herself when they watched a movie, to the personalized mugs that they always gave as gifts. Zeke's *Thou shalt not test me* Mug sat in the breakfast bar.

Jesus, his heart clenched because he knew Zeke must be going insane not knowing where Scarlett was, if she was okay, and if their baby was okay. He wished he could leave something, anything to let them know that she was safe, for now at least.

Who the hell knew what Dante had planned after the baby was born?

Callista had walked over to the fridge, looking at the pictures on the wall. Contrary to some vampire lore, vampires did appear in pictures, and they had a reflection in the mirror. She was looking at an old picture of him, Jazz, Malakai, and Zeke the night Dante's had opened, Jasmine popping champagne.

"You look sad in the picture when everyone is celebrating."

Did he? Dylan walked over to where Callista stood and looked at the picture harder. His smile was wide but it didn't quite meet his eyes. If he remembered right, it was only a few weeks after he had attempted death by sun and the dark cloud hadn't really left him, though he made a good effort to conceal it.

"I wasn't myself that night. Hell, there are days when I don't know if I'm me or someone else."

Callista shrugged, offering him a smile that seemed to make her eyes glow. "Today you are Dylan. That is what matters. One day at a time."

Fuck. He was royally fucked because he knew in his bones that he was falling in love with Callista. She knew him, saw him when he couldn't see himself, and it felt like torture. He wanted to tell her, to beg her not to go back to Dante and stay here, with them, but he knew that it would be futile.

"You know, we could use someone with your skill at Sicarius. You could come work with us."

Callista snorted as she roamed around the living area. "I think Death would have other ideas for me. The obscurum too. I have seen your sister's skill with a blade and no doubt she would like to carve little pieces out of me. I was not born to be surrounded with warmth and kindness and family."

Dylan felt the brunt of her anger as she whirled toward him, her green eyes glowing as she snarled, the emotions hitting Dylan square in the chest. "So, stop kissing me, vampire. Stop reaching for my hand and stop with any foolish notions that there is something is between us when there is not. I do what is necessary to ensure that you retrieve the scrolls. If that means pretending to feel, pretending to like being kissed by you, I will do it."

Her words said one thing, but her emotions said another and Dylan, he swallowed her emotions and yanked them from her, causing her to gasp and reach for the side of the sofa with one hand and then clutch her chest, her chest where Dylan had seen the tattooed mark.

Dylan thought about Dante, about all the symbols etched into his skin and it hit him: Dante had used the stolen magics to control Callista. The tattoo was not given to her by choice. It masked her emotions like one of those marks must mask Dante from Jazz's visions.

"Let us finish this." Callista strode to the door to the library, wrenching the door open and disappearing inside and Dylan was torn between whether to alert his family that he was here and keeping Callista safe.

With a snarl of frustration, he followed Callista into the library, taking the steps up two at a time, reaching the top as Callista descended the stairs, her eyes scanning the room. Even Dylan himself had to admit that Zeke's library was impressive. Over the years, he and Jasmine had a competition to see who could find the rarest books and scrolls for Zeke, hoping to cheer the man up. It was the only real time Dylan had felt happiness from the other vampire before he fell in love with Scarlett.

Zeke had spent centuries trying to understand what he had become and it was Dylan himself who had managed to find the pages of Lucifer. Zeke already had the original book, which detailed his fall from angel to king of hell, the birth of demons and Inferna. But the pages seemed like a load of gibberish to Dylan, and to Zeke as well, who thought you might need a key to decipher it.

Did Dante have the key? There was a hum of magic, dark magic on the torn-out pages when Dylan had retrieved them from inside an active volcano, the molten rock seemingly blocking the pages from being scried for, but it was a half-demon who had led Dylan to the pages, even though the demon refused to touch the pages, like he feared the wrath of Lucifer himself.

Dylan had always been reckless and had no issues putting his hands on the pages.

"Does the obscurum have any place he might hide the pages?" Callista asked, glancing around the room as she descended the last step.

"Why do you call him the obscurum? Does it make you feel better to call him a thing rather than a person? Is that why you call me vampire?"

Dylan jogged down the remaining steps, Callista turning to him with her expression blank and her arms folded defensively across her chest. "Ezekiel is the obscurum. It is fact. I call you vampire, because that is what you are. Same as Ezekiel. It is not my fault that for some reason it angers you to hear me call you vampire."

"Is it easier to pretend that we aren't real Inferna in this with feelings by referring to us as what we are?" He demanded of her, needed to hear the answer more than he cared to admit.

"Is it easier to pretend that I am capable of feelings by

calling me Blue and Callie, rather than accepting that I will never be like you?" Callista tossed back at him, her expression guarded.

Dylan recoiled like Callista had struck him, and he didn't need to feel her emotions to know that she spoke true. He had been a fool, a stupid fool who had grown tired of the endless revolving door of lovers and had started to crave what the rest of the family had.

Now was the time to be honest with himself. He wanted his own Keeva, his own Scarlett, or Roman. He wanted a partner to come home to, and he had been projecting that onto the harpy. But Callista was lying to herself if she thought that she could keep going on pretending that her emotions were non-existent. The truth would soon come out and the end result would mean Callista may end up just as heartbroken as him.

"Explain it to me then. Why is Zeke the darkness."

Callista shrugged her shoulders. "You ask too much of me. I cannot."

"Can't or won't?"

"Does it really matter, vampire? If I say that I won't ,will it turn the tide in your emotions and will you finally start seeing me as the enemy and not someone who is swayed by your good looks and charming tongue?"

Dylan smirked, taking a step forward. "You haven't seen how charming my tongue can really be yet, *Blue*."

He added an extra emphasis on the word blue so much so, that Callista rolled her eyes and sighed like she was already bored of this entire conversation. Dylan hadn't meant to get angry, but without anyone else's emotions to sense, he was too focused on his own, too focused on her.

"You forget, *vampire*," Callista retorted, walking away from him, turning away so he could not see her face. "I have watched you for some time. I have heard the heady moans from women and men as you used that charming tongue on them. I have watched their sweat-ridden bodies as you filled them and yet, it did not seem to make you happy. The same sad eyes you had in that photo. That is how I knew you were sad."

Dylan wasn't even shocked at the callousness in Callista's tone, he was just appalled at how much it described him, how deeply it hit home. Jesus, this was a shitshow. How the hell had they gone from kissing to arguing in the space of a couple of minutes? He was confused as all hell, not sure what was going on.

But they were wasting time and he doubted that JP would be able to keep up the façade for much longer. Molly would have changed back to herself the minute anyone tried to kill her, so he suspected they didn't have long before the place was crawling with Sicarius Security employees.

"Let's get this over with."

Dylan knew a few places where Zeke kept artifacts and things hidden, but after a quick search, Dylan realized that after they had discovered that Dante was searching for the pages, Zeke might have moved them to a place even Dylan didn't know about.

Or even worse. Zeke might be keeping them on his person.

Dylan wasn't liking the odds if that was true.

Pain pinched behind his eyes as he let Callista keep looking, going over to Zeke's desk, opening the bottom drawer, and pulling out a bottle of whisky Zeke stashed in there. Dylan opened the bottle, swigging from it, the burn at the back of his throat as he continued to drink.

"That is not being helpful."

"It's helping me, Blue. I think at my best when slightly intoxicated."

That wasn't true of course because the brunt of all his bad decisions had been made while drunk, but it would take a lot more than half a bottle of whiskey to get him even tipsy, much less drunk as all hell.

His chest constricted as he was reminded of the last staff night out that had had, when he, Jazz, and poor Scarlett had played drinking games and Scarlett had tried to keep up with him and Jasmine, getting so drunk she was dancing on counters and smacking Zeke's ass in front of all the staff.

It had been hilarious at the time ...but now, the poor woman was alone with a madman and he was here, trying to steal from her mate.

Dylan's stomach did a somersault, and he set down the bottle on the desk. "Zeke might have moved them off-site. They give off a sort of weird magic kinda feel and I don't sense them here."

The words had barely left his mouth when he suddenly got the tingly sense of the pages like he had when he retrieved them from the volcano. Callista had withdrawn her sword, bracing herself for an attack and when Dylan looked in the direction that had Callista's attention, he knew that they were in trouble.

CHAPTER TWELVE

Dylan

EZEKIEL COLLINS SEEMED TO APPEAR OUT OF THIN AIR, HIS expression murderous, and his eyes trained solely on the harpy who was glaring back at the menacing vampire like he wasn't a formidable foe. Dylan felt panic well in his chest at the same time he felt Zeke's white-hot rage boil his skin.

"How did you know?" Dylan asked him, knowing Zeke would understand the question he was asking.

Zeke took a step closer, his dark eyes tinged with red. "Jasmine. She had visions and told us - They are not safe in the tower; they are not safe from him. We assumed she meant Vindicta but never would we have even considered it was you we were not safe from."

The words hit him like a kick to the gut, shame washing over him that his family would think that he would betray them. He needed to make Zeke understand that he had done this to keep Scarlett safe.

"Are they okay?" Zeke demanded, striding forward, causing Dylan to glance at Callista but the harpy had not moved.

"They are unharmed, obscurum. I have a hellhound guarding her from Vindicta."

It was Callista that answered Zeke, her response drawing a growl from Zeke, his scarred lips curling into a feral snarl. "And why should I believe a goddamn word you say, harpy?"

"Because it will bring you some comfort, obscurum. Now, give me the pages so that your succubus might be released to you. My employer is not a patient creature."

"You want the pages, come and take them."

A coldness seeped into Callista's features as she angled her sword. "With pleasure."

Callista took a step toward Zeke, would have advanced more if Dylan hadn't stepped in front of her, the tip of her blade at centre mass. Her eyes narrowed, her ears twitching as Dylan held up his hands.

"Hang on a second, Blue. Just wait one goddamn second."

"You are in my way, vampire. Move."

Dylan was about to argue with her, but heard the safety coming off a gun a millisecond before Zeke fired a shot. Knocking the sword from Callista's hand, Dylan pushed her to the ground, letting out a roar as the bullet intended for Callista went through his shoulder. He covered Callista on the ground, even as she tried to shove him off, the wound on his shoulder burning.

"Please, Blue. Don't fight him."

"He just tried to kill me. And you. Get off me."

Dylan rolled off her, crouching in front of her, as Zeke tossed the gun aside like he didn't care that Dylan had been the one to absorb the blow. Callista kicked up her sword, and rotated it in her wrist as Dylan lunged for Zeke, not surprised when the much stronger, more motivated vampire swatted him away like he was a fly. His back hit one of the bookcases, the books tumbling all around him as he groaned. "Zeke, man, it's not what it looks like. Let me explain."

"I don't need your explanation, Dylan. This bitch kidnapped the woman I love and my unborn child. She will die."

"She's a prisoner too!" Dylan shouted at Zeke, but the vampire just laughed it off. Dylan was starting to panic, knowing Zeke could and would kill Callista, and in turn, his harpy could do the same to the man who was more a brother to him than the fiend holding Scarlett captive.

Dylan lashed out with his magic, hoping to suck the rage from the vampire, make him compliant and subdued. Zeke's eyes flared red, as Dylan's magic attempted to take from him, the other vampire not best pleased considering he took his gaze from Callista and focused on Dylan.

"Stop." Zeke demanded, stalking toward where Dylan was finally getting to his feet.

"I can't let you hurt her." Dylan said.

Understanding seemed to flicker in Zeke's eyes, yet it didn't stop his trajectory as Dylan reached out with his powers again, causing Zeke to stop for a brief moment before he readied to grab hold of Dylan.

Callista stepped in front of Dylan, shielding him from Zeke and she made no attempt to conceal her own anger. Dylan shuddered as she lifted her chin to look Zeke dead in the eyes.

"You will stand down, vampire."

Zeke snorted, sneering at Callista. "Make me, little girl."

Callista struck before Zeke had even finished the last syllable, plunging her blade forward and Zeke jerked back out of the path of the blade. Zeke spun, catching Callista with an elbow and she used the momentum to turn herself, leaping forward and slashing down, catching Zeke on the arm.

It was then Dylan realized that Callista was not fighting to kill Zeke; she was fighting to disable him. She wouldn't kill him because she understood he was just fighting for his family and that Dylan loved him. Callista was protecting him and it would get her killed.

Zeke dodged a few swipes of her sword, using his body to stay out of range and then striking when Callista was setting up another attack. His foot caught her in the stomach and she flew backward, letting go of her sword and rolling into a crouch.

There was murder in Zeke's eyes as he rolled up his sleeves and cracked his knuckles. Callista unsheathed her talons, making Zeke chuckle.

"Little girl, those talons are just foreplay to me. Nothing but a scratch. Surrender now and I will be merciful and leave you to rot in a cell for the rest of your immortal life."

"I desire mercy, not sacrifice. For I have not come to call the righteous, but sinners." Callista said in a loud voice and Zeke looked just as surprised as Dylan was.

"You do not get to toss scripture at me, harpy."

"Are we not both sinners seeking mercy, obscurum? I would rather choose death than be caged again. So cometh and deliver death to me if you so desire it. Sinner to sinner."

"Ask and you shall receive. Or as my good friend Kesha says, the party don't start till I walk in."

Dylan snapped his head toward the sound of Keeva's voice, despair coursing through him as Keeva came down the steps to stand beside Zeke, her gloveless hands poised ready to strike. Malakai was next, then Jasmine and Roman, their emotions hitting him like a tornado and he grabbed his head with both hands and slammed against the wall, swearing.

"Dylan!" Jasmine cried out, her pain causing him to moan, and as she made to come to him, he held up his hand to stop her.

"Just gimmie a damn minute!" It had been too long since he had been around a large group of people that he had forgotten the need to shield himself from their emotions. They all crushed down on him, making it too hard to wade through them and assign them with a particular person. People were calling his name, asking him if he was okay when he vomited on the floor, his knees threatening to give way when he felt a hand on his chest.

Dylan dropped his hands and just looked in Callista's eyes, held them as he blocked out the emotions, until it was just him and her in the library, her hand on his chest.

"You could rip my heart from my chest if you wanted to."

Callista snorted, rolling her eyes. "That would be very messy. I would cut off your head. Much cleaner."

Dylan barked out a laugh, resting his forehead against hers as she patted his chest. "I cannot let him cage me, Dylan. I will not."

Pressing a kiss to her forehead that had his family sucking in a breath, Dylan tried to reassure her. "No one is caging you, Blue."

Callista shoved him away, ducking as Zeke fired the gun again, Callista bolting across the room as Zeke fired shot after shot at Callista but she moved like a blur, coming back toward him and Dylan managed to grab her, forcing her behind him.

"He fucking bonded us together. If you kill her, you kill me."

Dylan wasn't entirely sure if the magic Dante had used to bind him to Callista worked like that, especially as she had shown no reaction to him getting shot, but it was worth using because he was almost ninety percent certain his family wouldn't want to kill him. Callista stabbed him with her talons at his back and he glanced over his shoulder and winked.

"Hey, I'm injured. Don't you forget I took a bullet for you."

"I have a feeling you will remind me quite often." She responded dryly, making Dylan laugh, much to the absolute shock of those who watched them, except for Malakai, who was looking at them with a masked expression.

"Why the fuck are we standing here listening to this bull-shit?" Keeva exclaimed, fury in her eyes. "I don't give a flying fuck if she's tied to Mac. I'm gonna melt her insides."

Callista kicked Dylan's legs out from under him, sending him crashing to the ground as Keeva managed to outrun Malakai, his brother trying to catch his fiancé around the waist, the petite banshee using all her skill to evade him, making a beeline for Callista.

Dylan saw Callista sheath her talons, leaning back as Keeva aimed a fist at her face. Callista straightened, then met Keeva punch for punch, no one wanting to get in between the fighting women as Keeva reached to place her palm on Callista but Callista manoeuvred sideways, kicking up her foot at the last minute and connecting with Keeva's jaw and Dylan's future sister-in-law stumbled backward, spitting blood onto the ground.

"I could do this all day." Keeva grinned, blood staining her teeth.

They circled one another, Keeva and Callista, ignoring everyone else in the room.

Are you well, brother?

Malakai's voice in his head felt like a welcome reprieve and he grabbed hold of that thought and concentrated on the connection that allowed Malakai to speak to him.

What is the harpy to you?

Well, that was a loaded fucking question, wasn't it? Dylan knew Callista was meant to be his and yet, admitting it would mean leaving those that he loved in this room because they would never accept Callista, even if it was for Dylan's benefit.

Ah...I see...

That was the last thing Malakai said to Dylan in his mind, as Zeke made to get involved in the fight, stopping only when Jazz's eyes flashed white and she told him to stop. Keeva stomped on Callista's foot, then swept Callista's other leg, knocking her to the floor, her back hitting it hard and she exhaled loudly.

Keeva was on her a second later, straddling her chest as she clamped her hands to the side of Callista's face and snarled. Dylan yelled Callista's name, the sound coming out pained, and Keeva lifted her gaze to Dylan and whatever she saw in his face made her mouth the words I'm sorry.

Time seemed to slow down and Dylan felt like he couldn't breathe, which was utterly stupid of him. Dylan had seen the remains of bodies after Keeva used her power on them, and waited for Callista to start screaming as Keeva boiled her blood from the inside out. It would kill him to see her suffer.

Dylan hadn't realized that he had snatched the gun from Zeke's hands until he was pointing it at Keeva, ready to put a bullet in his friend's head.

He had to protect what was his.

"Dylan...no..."

Malakai's emotions started to trickle through him but somehow, knowing his mate was about to die, Dylan shoved the emotions back at his brother hard enough to make Malakai grunt. Dylan was about to lose everything, his family, his life, the woman he loved, and he couldn't deny it anymore because here he was standing with a gun to his brother's mate's head.

It was taking too long, and Dylan stepped forward at the exact moment Keeva let loose a string of swear words and then yelled. "Jesus fucking Christ!"

There was a grunt of pain, as Keeva rolled off Callista and lay on her back, sucking in air, her green eyes focused on Dylan, but Dylan, even though he kept the gun on Keeva, his eyes scanned Callista for harm.

"You can lower the gun now, Dylan. Keeva's powers do not work on Callista."

Dylan's hand trembled as relief surged through his body, Malakai coming to stand beside him, reaching out to grasp the gun and take it from Dylan's hand. Malakai inclined his head, then went over to Keeva and held out a hand to help her to her feet.

"Bloody hell, Dylan. You were really gonna shoot me, weren't you?" Keeva asked as she rubbed her chest.

There was no point in denying it because he sure as hell would have. "Ya, I guess I was. Sorry."

Keeva came over and punched him in the shoulder, the one where Zeke had shot him and Dylan groaned. "Payback will be a bitch, brother."

And just like that Keeva had forgiven him and he almost sagged in relief, swallowing hard as Malakai went over to Callista, who was still breathing hard as she wearily watched Malakai. His brother held out his hand much like he had with Keeva.

"Ms. Rayne, I will not harm you."

Callista Rayne. Leave it to Malakai to find out more about his harpy then Dylan could get out of her, Callista taking the hand held out in offering and getting to her feet, as Keeva muttered beside him that she couldn't guarantee that someone else mightn't take a swing at her.

"Keeva." Dylan ground out, waiting until the banshee looked at him before he said. "Vindicta is her Angus. He purchased her from a cage when she was a child."

Angus McFergus had been the head of Keeva's scream and when his daughter had died when Keeva tried to save her from a fall, Angus had used that to make Keeva his own personal assassin and because Keeva was drowning in grief and guilt, only a child herself, she had let him.

If anyone understood what it was like to be a prisoner of circumstance, it was Keeva.

Another punch came to his injured shoulder as Callista turned on him. "How dare you tell these people my secrets. It is not your place."

"I thought harpies were meant to be emotionless?" Roman muttered, clearly amused.

"I guess this one's different." Jasmine replied grinning as if she already knew just how different Callista was.

Dylan remembered something important, glancing at Callista as he gripped her arm. "Is it only things about Vindicta I'm spelled to not talk about?"

The scowl on Callista's face told him everything he

needed to know. With his hand still on Callista's arm, Dylan spoke to Roman. "Ezra is working for Vindicta. He's the one who shot at you when me and Scarlett were taken. He's the one who took aim at Kai. Vindicta has him by the short and curlies according to him but he got paid well for it. He's the traitor."

"Son of a bitch!" Roman swore as he whipped out his phone and moved to the corner, no doubt calling his best friend Conor who, along with the rest of Roman's former squad had come to work for Sicarius. Except for Ezra, who Jazz had vetoed.

Callista whirled away from Dylan, snarling as she faced Zeke who stood in place seething with rage. "Give me the pages. Give me the pages now and I will deliver the succubus back to you."

"If your boss wants the pages, he can come get them from me himself. You scurry back and tell him that."

Callista's hands went to her hips. "He will cut the babe from her womb if I go back without the pages. He will leave her to bleed to death and then, he will order me to drop the succubus remains on your doorstep while her body is still warm. Give me the pages. Let me bring Scarlett back to you and I will do all I can to keep the child safe. If you do not do this you are signing her execution warrant yourself."

Dylan was so focused on making sure that Keeva didn't kill Callista that he had forgotten that even in this room filled with Inferna, Zeke was the biggest threat. A coldness danced along Dylan's spine as Zeke's lips curved into a sinister smile, the dagger appearing like magic in his hand before he slashed out.

Dylan had barely a second to spare as he put himself between Callista and Zeke's wrath, the dagger slicing across his neck, blood gushing from his throat as Callista recoiled in horror. Grasping at his neck, Dylan felt the cut start to knit back together as he turned to Callista, about to tell her that he was okay.

The harpy stared at him, her face paling, as she took in the blood that Zeke had managed to spill before the wound closed. For a moment, Dylan assumed that she was taken aback by how close she had come to dying because even Dylan didn't know if a harpy could heal from having their throat slashed, and Zeke had pulled back when he had realized it was Dylan.

Plus, the silver wouldn't do much damage to him.

But now, Callista was staring at the blood that soaked his skin, a glazed look in her eyes as she glanced down at her own hands, tilting her head before she said. "There is always so much blood."

Then Callista's eyes rolled back in her head and she crumpled to the ground, out cold as Dylan could do nothing but stand there open-mouthed, unsure what the fuck had just happened as Jazz came to stand beside him. "Huh, I didn't see that coming."

Jasmine's bemused look forced a chortle of laughter from Dylan, as he shook his head, embracing his sister as he admitted. "Neither did I, Jazz. Neither did I."

CHAPTER THIRTEEN

Callista

HER FOOTSTEPS MADE NO SOUND AS SHE MOVED THROUGH THE forest, her prey not too far ahead. The ground was crisp with frost, hanging to the blades of grass and glittering like spiderwebs. Her heart was racing with excitement and anticipation. It was the first time that she had been allowed to hunt by herself and if she came back with no food, then it would be a disappointment.

Callista had spent her early years disappointing her mother, she would not do it with the man who had taken her from the cage and shown her it was okay to have emotions.

Pausing and placing her hands on the trunk of a tree, the bark coarse under her fingers, Callista caught sight of the deer in the distance. Reaching back, she pulled an arrow from her quiver, nocking the arrow and with steady aim, pointed it at the deer.

It had taken Callista time to get used to killing animals for food. When she had been in Litochoro with the other harpies, food was provided to them, and she never saw the food before when it was alive. But with Dante, they travelled the world by foot and foraged in woods and forests and villages for food. She never went hungry and always had a bed to sleep in during the day.

They had been staying in a cabin at the far edge of this forest for months now and Callista would be happy if they never left. Dante had to travel to the village a few hours walk every night to feed, but that never bothered Callista. At first, when he left her alone, she feared that he would not return, and yet he always did.

Callista thought that after she had her first bleeding, that Dante would try and take from her, that he would want to rut and feed from her, but he never touched her in that way. He treated her like her sisters treated each other… like they had never treated her.

The wind picked up and strands of her blue hair escaped the braid and slapped against her face. The deer jerked its head up, its gaze snapping in her direction. Callista wasted no more time reminiscing, she let the arrow go and was already nocking another just in case her aim did not hit true.

She need not have worried so; Dante had trained her extremely well.

The arrow had hit the deer in the heart, killing the animal between one heartbeat and the next and Callista grinned, pumping a fist in the air as she celebrated her first solo hunt. She hauled the small deer up onto her shoulders, trying not to think of the blood that was dripping down her back.

Striding back through the forest, Callista could hear the sound of voices near the cabin, wondering who had come to pay them a visit. At any given time, a number of vampires had joined them as they travelled, most sired by Dante or friends he picked up along the way. Sometimes, other Inferna joined them also, but they never stayed for too long.

Stepping out into the clearing around the cabin, Callista spotted Dante talking to another vampire who glanced in her direction, his eyes reminding her of the Spartan, greedy and lustful, then Dante growled and the strange vampire dragged his gaze from Callista and back to Dante.

They exchanged a few more words as Callista set down the deer, her stomach rolling as she began to prepare the meat for cooking. Ever since she had killed the Spartan with her bare hands, the sight of blood seemed to trigger an emotional response and she was either ill or fainted. It had gotten better, over the last few years, but when she was stressed or the like, she still fell back to old habits.

Footsteps sounded behind her. Callista glanced over her shoulder to see Dante striding toward her, the other vampire gone, and her mentor tucked a package into his pocket. When he noticed that

Callista was looking at him, he grinned, his smile lighting up the dark of night.

"I knew you could do it!"

Callista felt her chest fill with pride as he ruffled her hair and then sat down beside her, silently taking the blade and finishing with the deer. Dante never told her who or why the other vampire had come to see him, nor did Callista ask. She was afraid that Dante might tire of her and get rid of her, should she not be useful to him.

Dante asked her to tell him how the hunt had gone, detail by detail as they prepared and ate their meal, morning not too long away. Callista went through each footstep, each subtle change of wind direction, each difference in the forest from the last time they had hunted together.

They ate their meal in silence, the crackle of the fire the only sound around as Callista ate the meat, admitting to herself that it tasted even better knowing that she had tracked and killed it all by herself. Dante was a lot quieter than usual, his handsome features highlighted by the blaze of orange flames that seemed to dance toward him.

"I might have to go away for a time." Dante told her suddenly, and Callista could hear the sadness in his tone.

"Do you know for how long? I could go with you." It pained her to think of him going off on his own and leaving her alone. She supposed that she had become accustomed to having him by her side, and even now that she was grown, she would still very much prefer to keep things as they were than to go out into the world by herself.

Dante shook his head, running his hands over his face. "This is a journey I must take alone. I wish I could take you with me. But I need you to promise me something. Can you do that, Callista?"

Callista nodded as Dante explained what he wanted her to do and bile crept up her throat as she nodded, promising to do as he asked. Tears filled her eyes and she covered her face with her hands, not wanting to show Dante just how scared and sad she truly was.

Cool hands rested over hers, gently taking them away from her face and she looked into green eyes and a sort of smiling face.

"Hush now, Callista. It will be okay. I must do this; I must claim what should have been mine all along. And never hide how you feel from me, okay? What did I tell you from the first moment we met?"

"My emotions are not a weakness. They are my biggest strength."

Dante cupped her cheek and grinned. "Exactly. Good girl. And I swear to come back to you. But if I do not, then you must go in search of the vampire I told you about. My brother. Do you remember everything I told you?"

Callista nodded. She never forgot a single word Dante told her. She committed it all to memory, especially when he had told her about his family in Ireland, the country of his birth, and told her to go find them if something happened to him and they would take care of her.

Dante spoke very little about his family, she didn't even know them by name, just by stories. She had heard the jealous tone when he spoke of his eldest brother, and yet, he still told her to go to him should she be in need of shelter.

But Callista would rather remain here, in this forest, far away from other Inferna or humans, safe in their cabin, content with her life now. It was the first time they had settled for longer than a few weeks and it was starting to feel like a home.

As the sun began to rise in the sky, Dante led her into the cabin, dousing the fire and she lay down on the cot beside the fire, the warmth making her feel toasty and content as she sighed. Dante shuttered the windows and doors, then sat downy in the chair beside her cot, taking the package from his pocket and even Callista could feel the wrongness emulating from it.

Callista lifted her head to study Dante as he scrutinized the book, his eyes scanning each line, each word. He seemed oblivious to Callista watching him, a strange hungry glint in his eyes. Then his head snapped up and he smiled.

"Go to sleep, little harpy. Tomorrow is a new night."

Snuggling into her bed, Callista closed her eyes, falling fast to sleep, not waking until long after the sun had set and she sat up, looking around the cabin for Dante.

But Dante was already gone… and he never returned.

In the end, it was Vindicta who came back for her, the man she knew was gone.

Callista bolted upright, sucking in air and reaching for a weapon of some sort but she had none on her person. Panic began to flood her chest and she struggled to breathe, not understanding where she was, as she was no longer in the library Her feet hit the floor and she swayed; her vision blurry. An arm snaked around her waist, and she snapped her gaze to see Dylan holding her, the stab wound cleaned and a lopsided smile on his face.

"Hey, it's okay. I got ya."

Dylan cautiously forced her to sit down on the couch and Callista was acutely aware that Dylan's entire family was watching them, half with unbridled amusement, the others looking like they were planning her death in various ways.

Her stomach rolled, and she knew she wanted to be sick. Dylan gave her a glass of bubbly white liquid, and she eyes him warily, but Dylan only laughed at her.

"It's just 7up. Keeva swears that it fixes every ailment. Speaking as someone who has had a number of hangovers, she might just be right."

Callista lifted the glass to her lips and took a sip, instantly feeling better so she took another much larger sip. It was delicious, the drink, reminding her of a lemon and lime punch they used to drink back in the place of her birth.

Dylan waited until she had drained the entire glass, then took it from her, his fingers lingering on hers before he set it down on the table in front of the couch. Her heart pounded in her chest as Dylan reached out and tucked her hair behind her ear. He leaned in, as if he wanted to kiss her, and Callista tilted her head up, wanting to feel his lips on hers even if it was the last time.

A throat cleared behind them, the growl rumbling in Dylan's throat making Callista smile just a little and that just made Dylan stare at her harder, and she frowned.

"Stop staring at me, vampire."

"I will when you tell me why you fainted at all the blood."

A muscle in Callista's jaw ticked, her gaze sliding to the Inferna sitting around the family table. Shifting uncomfortably in her seat, all she could manage to grind out was. "I told you that I do not like mess."

Dylan reached out to cup her face and Callista dodged, getting to her feet much to Dylan's dismay. Callista looked around for her sword, saw that the obscurum had possession of it, and from the grim expression on his face, Callista knew that retrieving it might just result in more bloodshed.

"As amusing as it is to watch my brother not being able to charm a woman, we have a few things we need to clear up."

The seer grinned as Dylan lifted his middle finger in her direction, reaching for Callista's hand, which she refused to take, and Callista could almost see the anger radiating from his skin.

Malakai rose from his seat, looking as unruffled as he always did, went to the kitchen and poured himself a coffee, taking a sip before he returned to his chair, but did not sit. "Callista, you have my word that after we have some answers, or whatever you can divulge, then you will be free to leave if you so wish. There will be no more bloodshed."

Callista narrowed her gaze, but Malakai simply arched an eyebrow and retook his seat. Brushing past Dylan, Callista felt him grab her arm, stopping her from going to the table.

"Take your hands off me, vampire." She demanded, ignoring the goosebumps that pimpled her skin.

"What the fuck did I do that you woke up pissed at me?" he snarled at her.

"I do not need you to rescue me. I do not need you to take a bullet or a blade meant for me. I do not need you exposing who or what I am to Inferna I barely know. Do you think it is easy for me to stand here, in front of people I have conspired against for my own reasons, baring my scars; my weaknesses?"

Dylan glanced down at the talon marks on her arms and then back up to her face, his mouth opening preparing to speak but Callista could not stop the words from tumbling from her own lips.

"I am the enemy, vampire. Don't romanticize a few stolen moments as anything other than that. I am not the banshee or the succubus to be welcomed into the fold by your family. I tried to kill most of them. I may still have to. If the Primus wishes to speak to me before I die, then so be it. But you must leave me alone. Just leave me the fuck alone."

Dylan blanched, whether it was the harshness in her tone or the fact that she had sworn, Callista didn't care. Tears pricked her vision and she stalked to the window, not wanting Dylan to see that pushing him away caused her pain. She heard something crash, and assumed that Dylan had broken something, yet she kept her gaze firmly on the world passing by outside.

She stayed like that for a time, then stiffened as Malakai came to stand beside her, his hands casually in the pockets of his tailored suit. He waited patiently, not saying a word until Callista huffed out a breath. "He needed to be told. He needed to understand."

Malakai did not respond, and that made Callista laugh, Malakai looking at her in surprise.

"I never knew your names until Vindicta ordered me to watch you. Yet I heard stories of you all, of the adventures you had as a family. Before we went to sleep, Dante would tell me about your childhood, your early days as a vampire. He spoke of his regret that ye had lost touch." Callista stole a glance at Malakai, his expression unreadable.

"I knew not your name, Primus. Only that were I ever in

need of shelter, it was to you I was to come. But I could not leave."

"So you stayed through it all."

"I did."

Malakai inclined his head like he understood, then looked back out the window at the city.

"We have met before, Callista. Though I don't blame you for not remembering."

Callista frowned, folding her arms across her chest. "We have not."

"You were in a market in Barcelona. Everyone was stepping out of your way. I was in the process of trying to figure out how to rescue the hellhound from its cage when you breezed past me, through the crowd and demanded possession of the hellhound. You used a dagger to send the demon back to hell, then freed the hound. Then I heard you say…"

"You are free now. No one will imprison you again." Callista finished for Malakai, who inclined his head.

"Exactly. You might not have recognised me then. I was going through a phase where I decided to not cut my hair or beard. It was not pleasant. I cannot pull off the long hair like my brother." Malakai offered her a smile, then sighed. "You can be free now too, Callista. We won't allow anyone to imprison you again, if you let us."

Callista wanted to thank him for his offer, to say that she could see now why Dante had told her to come in search of him should she need aid, however she could not. She had an obligation to the man who had freed her from the cage first and she would have to see it out to the bitter end.

"I cannot. I have an obligation that I must see through to the end, no matter the outcome. It is that obligation that keeps me at his side, nothing more, nothing less. I wish it was not so, but we cannot change how we ended up here."

"No, we can't. Come sit down for a while and let us see if we can see a way through that keeps us all alive."

Malakai strode away from her, taking his seat again as Keeva came up to her, holding out a hoodie. Callista took it, nodded her thanks then watched as Keeva lifted up her shirt and turned so Callista could see the scars on her back.

"Don't be ashamed of your scars. They prove you had the strength to survive. Took me a while to accept that but it's the truth."

Callista put on the hoodie, then asked. "You of all people should not be kind to me."

Keeva shrugged, inclining her head toward Dylan. "Dylan told me that you were kind to Scarlett despite everything. You left a hellhound to protect her. He said you don't want Vindicta to win any more than we do, so in my book, that makes us on the same team." Keeva peered over her shoulder, a genuine smile curving her lips. "They aren't a half-bad bunch once you get used to them. You and me, we are used to being alone or depending on one person. They can be a bit much. Dylan's got the biggest heart. He could be good to you, if you let him."

CHAPTER FOURTEEN

Dylan

"*YOU MUST LEAVE ME ALONE. JUST LEAVE ME THE FUCK ALONE.*"

Dylan paced back and forth as Malakai and then Keeva went to speak to Callista. He felt strung out, like he was a spring coiled, ready to snap. The coldness in Callista's tone had eclipsed the warmth in her smile just minutes before, and even while she had been unconscious, Dylan hadn't left her side, protecting her from his family. His own goddamn family and she just wanted to dismiss him.

Keeva had forgiven him for holding a gun to her head, told him she understood how single-minded alpha males got when their mates' were in trouble. It did little to ease the tension in him.

Callista craned her neck, then turned, heading toward the table, unsure of where to sit. Dylan was about to rush over to pull out her chair or some shit, when Jasmine patted the seat beside her, the harpy stealing a glance at him before she sat down beside his sister. The elevator opened and Roman came in, the werewolf already growling as he punched the wall, plaster coming away.

"Ezra took Réiltin. He had already gotten her by the time I was able to get in touch with Conor. Son of a bitch."

They all looked at Callista, who opened her mouth and tried to speak. When nothing happened, she sighed. "I cannot say."

Jasmine leaned forward, resting her chin in her hands.

"Silas told us. It didn't even dawn on me that Réiltin might be in danger. Vindicta needs the bones of a child who died before taking a breath, the scale of a dragon, the dust from a unicorn's horn, and the lost pages of the book of Lucifer. That means we have time to mount a rescue. He doesn't have the pages yet."

Roman came over and took a seat at the other side of Jasmine, resting his head on the table and Jazz ran her fingers through his hair to try and soothe him. Dylan was still looking at them when Malakai glanced up at him and asked him to take a seat.

Dylan sat down on the chair next to Callista, facing Malakai, glaring at Zeke who would not take his eyes off of his harpy. And that was what she was, no matter how much she wanted to deny it.

"Dylan, please?"

Dylan opened his mouth to tell them about Dante, but nothing but gibberish came out. "Fish tennis bear tea suitcase phone pants. Oh, for fuck sake!"

Slamming his fist down on the table, Dylan let loose another string of curses as he threw his hands up in the air. "I'm spelled not to be able to talk about any of it with anyone who hasn't seen him physically. I can't even bloody tell you."

Malakai flashed Dylan a toothy grin. "I might have a way around that."

His brother got to his feet and walked around to where Dylan was sat, then pointed at his head. "May I?"

"It's not exactly a picnic in there, Kai. You sure you want to wade in?"

Malakai reached out and patted his head like he used to do when they were younger, Callista watching the interaction with a little more curiosity than he expected. "I can take it."

Dylan nodded, closing his eyes as Malakai clasped the side of his head and Dylan felt the pulse of magic as Malakai looked inside. Projecting images into his mind, Dylan knew when Malakai finally latched onto the image of Dante, because Malakai hissed, severing the contact and Dylan opened his eyes to see Malakai standing beside him open-mouthed.

"No...it can't be him...are you certain?" Malakai asked him.

"Ya, it's him."

"Jesus, don't keep us all in suspense, tell us who Vindicta is." Jasmine demanded, frustration in her voice and Dylan couldn't blame her since Dante had been the one to put her into a deep sleep for almost a year.

"T-shirt bank money coffee bread brush spoon."

Dylan barked out a laugh at the puzzled look on Malakai's face and then laughed even harder when Malakai groaned. "Fucking hell that's annoying."

"If you, me, and Callista were alone, we could talk away about it. They have to see it for themselves for the spell to break."

Malakai looked at Jasmine. "I may need you for this."

Jasmine held out her hands, a silly grin on her face. "Feels like when the power rangers had to band together to fight the baddie. It's morphing time."

Laughing as nearly everyone on the table groaned, with even Zeke cracking a smile, Jasmine told them all to hold hands, Dylan's fingers finding Callista's as his other hand held on to Jasmine's. He snuck a glance at Callista, saw she had already closed her eyes, then he felt the tug of both Jasmine's and Malakai's magic as everyone around the table, through their combined magic, got to see that Dante was alive and the one who had it out for them.

He fucking loved loopholes to rules.

"No. No fucking way. He's dead. He's been dead for centuries. We saw his remains. I don't believe it. Dante is dead."

Zeke's head snapped around to Jazz, pain in his eyes.

They all knew that Jasmine had spent hundreds of years feeling guilty that she had disobeyed a warning and gone to see Zeke long before she was supposed to, her visions warning her that one of her brothers would die and then Dante had been killed. They had all seen his ashes. Or what they thought was his ashes.

"So, let me get this straight." Keeva said, twirling the strands of her red hair in between her fingers. "The brother that was supposed to have died long ago is actually still alive and the one who has it in for you because he was jealous that he was born with no power. And that pissed off brother is now brimmed full of magic?"

They all mulled over Keeva's assessment as they all let go of each other's hands, Callista pulling away her hand like his touch scalded her. Dylan slipped his hands under the table so that no one would see the way his fingers curled into fists.

"Dante's alive." Jasmine slumped down in her chair and Roman threw his arm around her, drawing her closer to him. "How did I not see this…see him?"

Dylan struggled to find any words that would comfort his sister, and from the look on Malakai and Zeke's faces, they were struggling with the revelation as well. Jasmine had started to cry now, Roman pulling her into his lap and she wrapped her arms around him and she cried silently.

"You did not see him because he used magic to conceal himself from your visions."

Jasmine lifted her head to look at Callista, who was staring at the table. "Explain it to me so I understand." Her tone was clipped, angry, not that Dylan blamed her. Yet, her face softened as she looked at the dismay on Callista's face. "Please, Callista. I need to understand how I missed it all this time."

Callista lifted her head, leaning back in the chair before she spoke. "The magics that Vindicta has, they are borrowed, stolen. He must keep it contained by etching symbols from the book of Lucifer into his flesh. The eye of Horus on the back of his neck protected him from you. He does dark things to ensure that it stays powered."

"I still don't understand." Jasmine told Callista, confusion on her face.

"Then I must show you."

Dylan watched as Callista swallowed hard, then pulled the zipper down on her hoodie. She shrugged out of the sleeve, then moved her vest to the side so that everyone could see the mark etched into her skin. It had faded even more from the last time Dylan had seen it, at least a shade lighter.

"Vindicta carved the mark into my chest with a ceremonial blade. Every so often, when the magics start to dwindle, he has to recharge it or the power does not do as it was intended and keep them all contained."

"What the hell would Dante want to keep contained so badly that he would mark you like that?" Zeke ground out, his eyes not leaving the mark on Callista's chest and Dylan found himself growling possessively, so much so that Callista rolled her eyes and righted her clothing.

Her green eyes held Zeke's, answering his question directly. "My emotions. It is why you cannot hear my heart race or Dylan cannot tell what it is that I am feeling. The magics wear off and then I must endure the pain of having it redone. It has been on my skin for so long that it is now a part of me, never to be erased only muted. He changed me forever more."

Dylan surged to his feet, wanting to kill somebody, he wanted to kill Dante. He wanted to wrap his hands around his brother's throat and squeeze until his head popped off.

"Forgive me for asking, but you do feel emotions, right? The mark just keeps them hidden?"

He could have kissed Kai for asking Callista and it made him sit down again, eager to hear her answer. Callista's fingers fidgeted with the zip of her hoodie, her eyes closing and staying closed as she answered Malakai.

"At first no. The power was so strong that I did not feel a thing. I was empty, hollow. I knew that I should be feeling but by the time the mark started to fade, Vindicta had already begun to set his plan in motion. When he noticed me slipping, when he noted me feeling, he would redo the process and by the time it was done, it hurt so much, I welcomed the numbness. The older I got, the less it took and I have hidden the marking's failing for the last few months so that I am myself at the end."

Jasmine slid off of Roman's lap, resting a palm on Callista's shoulders about to say something when her body jerked and her eyes went snow white.

"At least it's not freaky black this time." Keeva remarked as Dylan eyed his sister wondering when the hell his sister's eyes had gone black?

"Eeny, meeny, miny, moe, catch a traitor by the toe. The tower is breached, it is not safe. Betrayal comes along in waves. The truth can no longer set them free. Death is the catalyst; the babe's cries signal the end. The war of hearts to tip the scales, the flames to consume."

Jasmine sucked in a breath, her eyes returning to their normal green as she looked to the ceiling. "Bit fucking late now for you to start showing me shit I already know!"

"I thought Ezra was the traitor?" Roman asked Jasmine, blatantly ignoring Jasmine's conversation with the fates.

"Sounds like we might have another traitor in our midst." Zeke remarked, glaring at Callista, who had opened her eyes during Jasmine's vision.

"If I wanted to betray you, obscurum, then I would have pretended to be all warm and fuzzy and lead you all into a trap. Or I would not have held back when you and the banshee attacked me. I could have killed either of you many times."

Zeke got to his feet, his chair scraping along the floor so hard Dylan was sure it would leave a mark. The other vampire grabbed Callista's sword and tossed it at the harpy, who caught it with ease as she rose.

"Then let's go. Do your worst." Zeke snarled as Callista moved around the back of her chair for space and then tested the blade in her hand.

Aggression and anger and everyone's emotions suddenly slapped Dylan hard in the chest and then everyone started talking all at once, making his head feel like it was going to explode. Zeke was sizing Callista up, cracking his knuckles as he moved toward her and Dylan snapped.

"Stop! Just fucking stop thinking and feeling and trying to kill each other. Just fucking stop!"

He felt a pulse of his magic lash out, blinding him for a second as Dylan seemed to grab hold of every emotion in the room. It pulsed through him, making him shudder, unable to see but it was like each individual person had a colour to their emotions.

Zeke's anger burned a vicious shade of red, while Callista's looked like the flames of a fire. Malakai was a calm blue, like the waves of an ocean. Jasmine's pain flickered with shades of purple, Roman's love for his sister as big and green as the forest he had his cabin in. And Keeva, she was a ball of red and blue and greens, at war with her emotions.

He had them all in his mind and he could rip them all from them. He could heal them all, take away all their emotions and take them into himself. He could end their suffering.

Dylan realized then that would make him no better than Dante, who had smothered Callista's emotions and taking away her choice to feel life and all its wonders and all its evils. He was not Dante and he never would be.

Somehow, Dylan cut the chord on his magic, all his strength leaving him as he put his head in his hands and groaned, blinking hard to try and regain his vision.

"What the hell was that?" Jasmine shouted at him; her eyes wide.

"When did your eyes go black?"

"I can stop time now." Jasmine boasted, looking smug as all hell when Dylan looked at her.

"She can," Malakai confirmed, his lips tugging into a sly smile. "For about thirty seconds. Then she loses concentration."

"Hey, I managed to do it for a whole minute yesterday."

Callista was watching the exchange, must have made a face because Roman grinned at her. "You get used to it. This is mild compared to usual. They must be easing you in."

That seemed to settle the unease that had lodged in his chest, because he thought, just for a minute that his family might accept Callista. He needed them to be okay with her.

Fingers touched his hand and Dylan looked up to see Jasmine's white eyes. "You don't have to choose. You won't have to choose."

The words were whispered as everyone took their seats again, Callista keeping the sword by her side this time just in case Zeke decided to have another go at her. Malakai was looking at Callista, and for once, Dylan would have loved to have Malakai's power to be able to know exactly what he was thinking.

Malakai glanced at Dylan, lifting his brows and Dylan chuckled, knowing his brother had heard the thought. Dylan told him to fuck off in his head and Malakai laughed then, causing Keeva to elbow him in the chest.

"No fair having conversations with each other in your heads. It's just rude."

Malakai apologized, dropping a kiss to her lips that seemed to appease Keeva, her cheeks reddening as Dylan burst out laughing. "No fair having conversations with each other in your heads. It's just rude."

Keeva flipped him off, and Dylan wished they could stay

here, in this bubble, and not face whatever was coming next. But he knew that the showdown with Dante was coming and it was coming soon.

"Callista, would you mind explaining to us how you happened to become our brother's companion."

Callista shifted in her seat and Dylan reached under the table to squeeze her knee, her gaze darting to him. Glaring at him for a heated minute, she turned her focus back to Malakai.

"When I was born my mother said she knew I was different. Instead of being born silent, entering the world with no emotions, I cried and cried until my mother thought it best to smother me. During her pregnancy, my emotions had affected her so she could not bring herself to do it. She probably regretted that long after."

Callista lowered her lashes, inhaled a breath, then opened her eyes again and Dylan listened intently as she spoke. "After I killed a Spartan, my mother decided to sell me on, for I was bringing shame to my Nest. She kept me in a cage to sell me to the highest bidder. Dante purchased me and set me free."

Dylan moved his hand up her leg and rested it there, hoping to offer her some comfort.

"Dante trained me to fight, to hunt, to protect myself. He taught me to read and how to speak different languages. It was hard learning English at eleven but he spent hours teaching me. We travelled the world with one another for centuries, searching for treasures. I did not know what he searched for or I might have been able to stop him.

We took up residence in a cabin with a forest and a village that was far enough away that I did not fear the humans. Dante started to change. He was distracted, less quick with a smile. One night a vampire came and gave him a book and I went to sleep and Dante was gone when I woke."

Callista cleared her throat and Dylan wanted to do what

Roman had done with Jasmine and pull her into his lap and comfort her. He wanted the permission to do it without question.

"I waited and waited for years and Dante did not come back. Then, when I could not stand the aloneness anymore, I went in search of him, and yet, I still could not find him. I returned to the cabin and there was a stranger waiting for me. Vindicta."

There was a sadness in her tone, like she had lost someone important to her. He was so focused on Callista that her words hadn't registered, they hadn't held any meaning to him but something had struck Malakai because he leaned forward in his seat.

"Why do you speak of our brother like he is two different people?"

CHAPTER FIFTEEN

Callista

"BECAUSE IT IS THE TRUTH."

Callista did not understand the weight of the secrets she had been carrying for so long, until speaking of her past a moment ago. And she could have rejoiced when Malakai had noticed how she referred to Dante as one person and Vindicta as another. All her reports had told her that he was sharp and observant, and this proved it.

"What the hell are you talking about?" The vampire to her right demanded, his grip on her thigh tightening and Callista found she was not entirely displeased by it.

Malakai tapped his chin. "I noticed that when Callista spoke of Dante, in the now, she referred to him as Vindicta. However, when she spoke of her past, it was always Dante. Am I on the right track?"

"Does this have something to do with what happened back at his lair? When for a second, Dante sounded all confused?"

Callista reclined in her chair, resting her hands on the table. "Yes. That was Dante. The rest of the time, it has been Vindicta that has been speaking to you all."

"Okay, back up." Keeva interjected, a look of confusion on her face. "For those of us not as smart as my soon to be husband, you're going to have to explain it in idiot terms for me. I'm all kinds of confused."

It would be hard to explain it all, when it was not something that she understood herself for Vindicta was not very forthcoming with information. Dante had always spoken to her honestly, as honestly as he could but Vindicta only used her for gain.

"I will try and make it more clear, however, I do not understand it all myself." Callista told Keeva, then glanced at Dylan, who gave a brief nod of his head, encouraging her to continue.

"Dante always wanted to find a way to harness magic. He wanted to understand how he could have been born first, with similar parentage, and not have a sliver of magic in his genetics. He hated feeling like he was inadequate, less than his siblings and it ate at him. It was his only flaw, his envy."

"We never treated him as less than us. That was all in his head."

"Indeed." Callista agreed with Jasmine. "But he became obsessed over the decades. First, he found the ceremonial blade believed to have been Lucifer's when he was still an angel, lost from his hand when he was cast to hell. Then he found pages from the book of Lucifer, some scattered throughout the world. Even without having all of the book, the pages held spells and secrets no mere Inferna was ever meant to wield."

"How did he fake his death?" The seer asked her quietly, as if she needed the answer to that particular question before she could start to comprehend what Callista was saying.

"You and he had been estranged for some time, and I was still a child at the time so I did not understand. Dante told me that he wanted to test the spells in the book and because of that, he said he wanted to play a trick and see if you would think him dead. I helped him etch the eye of Horus into his neck and he dressed another vampire in his clothing, setting him alight at the time he knew ye were coming to find him. You saw the ashes of the vampire and assumed it was Dante. When the mark proved effective, he began testing more and more and he became obsessed with finding the book."

Callista looked at the obscurum, wetting her lips before she continued. "One of Dante's mercenaries located the book in a monastery in Ireland. They ripped the place apart to secure the book not knowing the impact it would have. It was that mercenary who made you a vampire."

The vampire glared at her; his eyes almost black but his body trembled as he regarded her.

"Does he still live?" the vampire ground out so hard she heard his teeth grind.

"No," Callista told him. "In my search for Dante, before I knew what he had become, I tracked him down and killed him. It may not comfort you to know he suffered a great deal before I killed him, once he told me that he was responsible for taking away the only father I had ever known."

"How the fuck can you calmly sit there and tell us that Vindicta is your father?" Keeva snarled at Callista and she understood all their anger.

"Vindicta is not my father nor is he a father figure. Dante was. Now if you would all stop deviating from the story then maybe you might stop asking me questions, I am already trying to answer."

The vampire to her right snorted, biting his lip to stop from laughing. Callista sighed, rubbed her temple, the start of a migraine making her head start to hurt. Her stomach rumbled, making Dylan dart to his feet.

"Shit, I forgot you need to eat and that." Dylan looked at Malakai as he walked toward the fridge. "How the hell do you remember to feed Keeva?"

Keeva looked mildly insulted, like she was being referred to as Malakai's pet human, and Malakai laughed, kissing the banshee's throat. "Believe it or not, Keeva can feed herself. She would tell me if she was hungry."

Dylan hmmmpt at Malakai's response, drawing a chuckle

from the other vampire. Coming back to the table, Dylan shoved a bar of chocolate toward her as well as a packet of crisps. He also set a bottle of 7up in front of her.

"Thank you." Callista said, feeling her chest expand as Dylan grinned at her. To mask her feelings, she opened the bar and nibbled at it, smiling. "Dante was the first person to give me treats. To give me chocolate. Anytime I acquired a new skill, he would return with something sweet for me. I had forgotten, until now. It has been a long time since I have had something sweet to eat."

Dylan pulled his chair closer to hers, leaned his head against her shoulder, and refused to be moved when she elbowed him. Huffing out a breath, she washed down her chocolate with a drink of the 7up before she continued.

"The final version of the book contained spells created in Hell. One such spell included the means to summon a demon from Hell. But not just any kind of demon. A Prince of Hell."

Malakai swore, as the obscurum looked at her like she was insane, the rest of the table just staring at her, their jaws almost hanging opening comically.

"The spell calls forth one of the Prince's that is linked to the sin you carry most in your marrow. Dante could never shake his jealousy and envy toward you all. Therefore, when he had gone through the transformation, when he had completed all the tasks set out, he summoned a Prince of Hell and it was Leviathan who answered."

Every Inferna around the table knew the demons of Hell as much as the angels of Heaven. Leviathan was a Demon Lord, one who presided over the sin of Envy and was one of the Seven Princes of Hell that rules Hell. He was also known as the gatekeeper of Hell itself.

"The thing he wants to open. It's Hell, isn't it?" the seer asked.

"Yes. He wishes to use Dante to gather the items needed

to open a gateway so that he can walk as himself in the human world. He wants to become its ruler."

"Your gods mean nothing to me, Dylan. I bow to no mere token gods. I am becoming a god. That's what he said to me. Vindicta or Leviathan wants to become a god and unleash demons on the human world."

"But how is he doing that, isn't he locked away in Hell?" Keeva asked and Callista did not have to answer because the Primus had already figured it out.

"Possession. He offered Dante power in return for use of his body for a time while he figured out how to open the gate."

Callista inclined her head, frowning. "Five hundred years. Dante let himself be possessed for five hundred years and I have stood by Vindicta to return the favour to the man who once set me free."

"But why call himself Vindicta. Why not pretend to be Dante all along?"

It was a question from the wolf. "He explained it to me once, when I asked the same of him. He told me that Lucifer had once shed his angelic past when he was cast out of heaven, becoming Lucifer and leaving Samael behind. Vindicta told me that it was only right that he too shed his demonic name in favour of one fitting a god. Hence Vindicta."

"Dante was never that stupid, right? He was never so stupid that he fell for all this, for what? A taste of power. I would have given him mine, if I could have, willingly." Dylan insisted.

"By the time Dante realized the mistake he had made, it was too late. So he became Vindicta, trapped inside his body and mind while Vindicta set forth his plan. But somewhere in the last hundred years, the envy and jealousy Dante felt has trickled into Vindicta and that was when he started to focus on seeking vengeance for what Dante saw as slights against him."

"Are you telling me that a Prince of Hell, possessing their supposedly dead brother's body, is holding my woman and my child hostage?" Zeke snarled at her.

"Yes."

Zeke lurched to his feet, picked up his chair and tossed it across the room, the furniture hitting the wall and splintering apart with the force of the impact. Callista could not blame the vampire for his reaction, because knowing that the man planning on slaying your child was a monster from the bible that you once coveted was extremely alarming.

"So, Vindicta or Leviathan or whatever has decided to go all Buffy super villain and try and open a hellmouth. Like, "From beneath you, it devours" and all that?" Jasmine asked Callista.

"Vindicta is the Gate to Hell." Malakai said, running his hands through his hair. "I might not know the bible as well as Zeke but Vindicta is referred to as the hellmouth. Once he has enough power and the pages, he just has to open his mouth and hell will reign on the human world."

"But why possess Dante? Why not just open a gate himself and come at us?" Roman offered, pulling the seer in tighter.

"He can't. He and one of the lesser Princes, Astaroth, almost started a war in Hell and Lucifer placed him in his own realm, away from Astaroth, in order to put an end to it. He would need a spell of Lucifer's own creation to set him free. Dante summoned a Prince of Hell and that was the opening Vindicta needed. We will kill the vessel and send him back to where he fucking belongs."

Panic and fear pushed Callista to her feet at the decisiveness in the obscurum's tone. "You cannot. Killing the vessel means killing Dante. He might mean little to you but he is in there, trapped."

"It is what he deserves. He summoned the Prince and now

he must suffer the outcome of it. The man you knew has been dead and gone for centuries. It is time his body joined him."

Callista was no longer trying to hide her emotions as she slammed her fist down on the table. "Then you condemn him to a lifetime of suffering. Sending Vindicta back will take Dante's soul with him and he will be tortured till the end of days. You were once a man of God, can you of all creatures not offer redemption for a mistake?"

Callista flinched at the cold smile on the vampire's scarred lip. "I had my redemption. Scarlett was my redemption as was Grayce. Vindicta and Dante are trying to take that from me. God abandoned me long ago, harpy. Just like Dante abandoned you."

Callista snapped her face to the right so Ezekiel could not see the pain on her face. It was true. Dante had left her. He had chosen this new path without considering Callista in any of it. And yet, though it hurt her to hear the words, to accept them, Callista could not abandon Dante to Vindicta.

"I think we all need to take a minute and calm down before we decide on a plan."

Callista was almost relieved to have Malakai step in and call a halt to what may have turned into a bloodier argument. Picking up her sword, Callista stepped out from the table, keeping her eyes from the handsome vampire who was watching her with weary eyes.

"I should go." Callista said as everyone started to rise, giving Dylan her back when he leapt to his feet.

"No."

She felt him come up behind her, and she spun, angling the sword at his throat. She expected him to hold up his hands in defeat, but instead, he leaned into the blade, the scent of copper filling the air.

"You do not get to order me about, vampire."

"And you don't get to walk away just like that, Blue."

They glared at each other, neither willing to be the first to back down. The intensity of it, the aggression of the vampire in front of her and her own fury flushed her body, tightening her lower half and making her want to bite the vampire for being such an insufferable ass.

"What just ran through your head, Blue?"

Callista blinked at the words, reminded of the first time she had considered getting naked and rutting with the vampire and from the crazed grin on his face, he was also reminded of it, because he leaned further into the sword, inhaled, and whispered. "Your scent changed."

Withdrawing her sword with a snarl, her talons elongating, Callista pivoted and headed for the elevator, looking to escape. It was obvious that she would not be leaving with pages from Lucifer's book and would have to face Vindicta's wrath herself. She would ensure that Scarlett was protected, and would take the brunt of his anger herself.

"Wait!"

Callista froze at the sound of the seer's voice, taking her time to turn back around. The seer was pacing back and forth, her eyes the colour of milk, her head moving like she was hearing a song in her head. No one else seemed overly worried, and, it seemed knowing Vindicta's true identity had removed any blocks Vindicta had tried to impose on her.

"Tick tock, tick tock, no more time left on the clock. Two truths and a lie, one of them must die. Eeny, meeny, miny, moe, catch a traitor by the toe. Sneaky sneaky, vampires. Even sneakier harpy. Eeny, meeny, miny, moe, catch a traitor by the toe."

The seer's eyes returned to their normal shade of green and she staggered, her mate catching her in case she was going to fall. She rubbed her temples, lifting her gaze to Callista, locking gazes before she said. "Zeke, give Callie the pages."

Callista frowned, first at the seer ordering the obscurum to give her the pages, and also by the nickname. The seer winked at her, glancing back at the vampire she thought of as a brother.

"I would not willingly ask you to give Callie exactly what Vindicta wants but this is the path we must travel on. Please, Zeke, my brother. Please give Callie the pages."

It took a few minutes before the hulking vampire was spurred into motion, halting when Dylan grabbed his elbow and the two seemingly shared a silent conversation before Dylan let him go and Ezekiel Collins stood before her and she had to tilt her head up to look into his dark eyes.

"Every instinct in me is screaming at me not to give you the pages. That handing them to you is as good as if I am killing Scarlett and the baby myself. I don't trust you, harpy, but I trust Jasmine and if she tells me that I need to hand over the pages to you, I will. Do not make me regret this."

The obscurum reached inside his jacket and withdrew the pages, slow to hand them over to Callista, yet he did, with Callista aware that everyone was watching the exchange. The moment the papers were in her hand, Callista made to leave, her mission complete.

Ezekiel grabbed her arm, holding on tight. "I was like you once. Convinced I was content with being alone. I became complacent. It was easier to push others away so I didn't feel anything other than the darkness, other than the hatred for myself. Then these idiots wormed their way inside my heart and I found Scarlett. Are you happy with your life, harpy? Are you content with being alone?"

Leaning in closer, the obscurum continued. "The lure of being alone can be debilitating. Don't let your life pass you by. Be honest with yourself and ask is this what you really want?"

He released Callista then and she stumbled, struggling to find her footing. Was she content with being by herself? When Dante had first left, Callista had hated the silence, the lack of conversation. And yet she was altered now, changed that perhaps alone was all she deserved. It would be easier for them all if she simply did what was required of her and then vanished.

Callista lifted her eyes, clashed with determined blue-green eyes that told her that he was not about to let her walk away from him without a fight and Callista wondered if this was how a person felt when they had someone to fight for them, when she was tired of fighting for herself.

"Callie, Dylan needs to go with you. Dylan has to go back with you."

Callista wanted to pull her gaze from Dylan's, to glare at the seer for not telling them they needed to separate and she almost groaned at the feral smile on Dylan's face as he remarked. "Guess, you're stuck with me, Blue. There's no getting away from me now."

In all honestly, Callista was not sure if that was meant as a threat or a promise.

Probably both.

CHAPTER SIXTEEN

Dylan

DYLAN DECIDED HE OWED JASMINE A MASSIVE CHRISTMAS present if they survived a Prince of Hell. The look of undiluted fury in Callista's expression was enough to make him want to strip her naked and lay her out on the table and devour her. It must have read in his own face because Malakai called him aside, leaving Callista alone with a very excited Jasmine, who was asking her all these questions about her talons.

Malakai clasped him by the shoulder, taking him as far out of earshot as possible, but Dylan knew that most of the Inferna in the room could probably still hear them.

"She is your mate."

It wasn't really a question, much more a statement, but Dylan nodded his head anyways.

"Callista may not return your feelings, Dylan. What was done to her…what Dante or Vindicta did to her, she might not have the ability to feel the same way as you do. If you consummate the mating, if you let yourself fall, then you may spend your life trying to find her if she should disappear."

Malakai wasn't telling Dylan this to hurt him. He was telling him the truth to try and prepare Dylan in case Callista vanished after they either managed to figure out how to send a Prince of Hell back to where he came from, or they failed and she fled to try and keep herself safe.

"When did you know Keeva was it for you?" Dylan asked Malakai.

His brother looked over to where his banshee was standing, and as if she felt his eyes on her, she lifted her head and smiled warmly at Malakai, rolling her eyes when Malakai replied to Dylan. "The moment she broke in and tried to kill me. I knew there and then she had to be mine."

Dylan laughed, and then Callista turned her eyes toward Dylan and Malakai, her eyes narrowing when he smiled at her. She quickly averted her gaze, shifting her balance like she was eager to get on with things.

And considering the way Zeke was glaring at her, Dylan didn't blame her.

"Even if we get Scarlett back, even if we end Vindicta. Zeke will never forgive her. I won't be the reason why this family falls apart, Kai. Those months when Jazz and me had that argument over that prick almost killed me. I can't lose ye, Kai."

Clasping the side of Dylan's neck, Malakai lowered his forehead to Dylan's. "I'll speak with Zeke. Let us see this through. You know, you were always the one I worried about the most. I may not have let it show, but I did. I always imagined that you would end up happy with a woman like Scarlett, soft, kind-hearted. I should have known you'd follow the family line and fall for a woman with balls of steel."

Dylan hugged his brother, kissing him hard on the lips as Malakai laughed, pushing him away. They walked back over to the rest of the group, Dylan reaching for Callista's hand, growling when she smacked it away.

You sure you want to do it this way?

Malakai spoke into his head as Dylan strode over to the fridge, taking a bottle of blood and draining it as he watched Malakai continue to have a conversation with everyone else while still speaking telepathically to Dylan. It always impressed him.

Careful now, or you'll make me blush.

Dylan coughed, almost choking on his drink at the teasing tone in his head and he really wanted to flip his brother off, but that would give the game away and Malakai knew it, his lips twitching like he was trying his hardest not to laugh.

You're a bastard, Kai. Ya, it might be the only advantage we'll have and we need every one we can take. Tomorrow night we'll go back.

Malakai inclined his head and then he somehow managed to distract the rest of the group while he went about with the secret part of their plan. He wouldn't tell Callista about it though, because as committed as he was trying to figure out if things could work out between them, she had her loyalty to Dante, to the man who raised her, and if push came to shove, Dylan wasn't sure she would put him ahead of that.

"We should go."

Dylan turned to see Callista behind him, that unreadable mask on her face. Not waiting for Dylan to answer, she walked right to the elevator, then stood rigidly as Dylan went and embraced his family, felt Callista's eyes watching the interactions.

When it came to Zeke, Dylan stood in front of him, pushing as much intention into his eyes as he could. "I will bring them back to you. No matter the cost."

Zeke didn't say anything, but his eyes looked like he was trying hard not to cry, not to be all possessive male vampire and demand that Callista take them back to the lair now. Dylan wasn't sure how much of the plan he knew, but hopefully that he knew enough.

"Callie! Wait a second."

Dylan left Zeke be, making his way over to where Jasmine was in the process of hugging a very stiff-looking Callista, with Jasmine leaning in to whisper in the harpy's ear, Callista's eyes widening. Jasmine let Callista go, grinning from ear to ear as she winked, then bounced her way back over to the rest of the family.

Handing Callista her sword sheath as they stepped into the elevator, he pressed the button to go down, and Callista put her sword along her spine. She kept her gaze averted, not looking him in the eyes, and for the first time in his life Dylan really wished that he could get a read on what someone else was feeling.

"Your family adore you." She said as the elevator reached the underground carpark.

Dylan grinned, stepping outside, but taking the time to peer over his shoulder at her. "Well, I am adorable. So, it's not really hard."

His harpy rolled her eyes, then she followed him out. They had already discussed the part of the plan where they pretended to have had a bloody altercation inside so that Dante wouldn't know that anything else was amiss, in case he had other spies watching him and Callista. They would sneak back into the tunnels and spend the day at the apartment so that Malakai and the others could do as much research as needed on how to banish a Prince of Hell.

"You need to hit me."

Dylan reared back, Callista sighing at his reaction. "We spoke of this. If Vindicta has other minions watching us, then we need it to look like I've been bloodied. Therefore, you need to hit me."

"I can think of other ways to make you bleed." Dylan said, his tone husky, his fangs elongated as Callista held out her wrist.

Dylan crowded her, backing her up against the wall, his hands braced on either side of Callista's head, her hand now planted firmly on his chest. Leaning in, he inhaled her scent, delighted when she shivered.

"Would the wrist not suffice?"

In answer, Dylan nipped at her pulse, felt Callista's body soften against his and the harpy tilted her head to give him better access. His gums ached, his mouth watered as Dylan flicked his tongue over her skin, tasting salt and feeling the beat of her pulse in her throat.

When Callista's free hand snaked up to cup the nape of his neck, Dylan pierced her skin, felt Callista jerk, hiss from the bite, but the moment he started to suck, to swallow her blood, her talons dug into the back of his neck, and if Dylan had no control, he would have tried to fuck her against the carpark wall.

Reluctantly, and aware that they might have an audience considering he had already taken down the security camera loop when Callista had fainted, Dylan retracted his fangs, letting a little of Callista's blood drip down her throat, and his erection became embarrassingly uncomfortable in his pants, as he licked at the wounds to close them.

Callista pulled her hands from his neck so suddenly that he thought her talons might rip through his flesh but the harpy had already sheathed them. His own blood trickled down his neck, the wounds already healed. Dylan clashed eyes with Callista for the briefest of moments, then she shoved him out of the way and jogged up the slope.

Dylan threw his hands up in the air, frustrated as all hell, but then he ran after Callista, her blue hair like a beacon in the dead of night. They went into the building across the street, going down into the tunnels once more, and Dylan knew that if they survived all this he would need to spend days figuring out where every single hatch led and make use of it.

Callista remained quiet as they travelled, not even commenting when Dylan shrieked at a rat that ran across his foot. Her shoulders were rigid, her body tense, and she refused to speak at all so Dylan gave up trying. It was like with every step they took back to Vindicta, Callista was disappearing before his eyes. He wanted her to be the sarcastic, sardonic harpy who gave as good as she got from him.

Rounding the corner, Dylan wondered how he could broach the subject of asking Callista to stay with him. To tell her that she was his mate, and despite not knowing her for all that long, he was in love with her. He knew it was insane, but he was an empathic centuries-old vampire whose supposedly dead brother was now having a Prince of Hell as a house-guest in his body. Falling in love was the easiest part of all of this madness.

But Callista had spent a lot of her life believing her emotions were a weakness, and Dylan himself had felt that his ability to know exactly what others were feeling was his biggest liability, but now, he realized he had been using his ability to ignore what his own feelings were. And yet, with Callista, someone he couldn't read clearly, it just made him want to take the time to figure her out.

The harpy stomped her way through the tunnels at a hasty pace, and she gripped the ladder so tightly that he was certain he heard the metal groan. If Dylan didn't know any better, he'd think she was pissed off with him.

When Dylan let them into the apartment, she stormed off into the bathroom, leaving Dylan standing there perplexed. He went into the kitchen and threw together a quick meal, taking time to clean the blood from his neck with a washcloth. He had the urge to go to the bathroom and check on her, but he felt that would be too much too soon. Dylan didn't want to push too hard in case he freaked her out by being too extra.

It reminded Dylan of the one time he thought he'd been in love, years ago with a countess who had been so obsessed with him, with becoming a vampire and retaining her good looks. Deep down, Dylan had known that he hadn't really loved Adela, but she made him feel special, loved, and he had blocked out his own emotions in order to drown in hers.

It had been at the same time that Jasmine and Thorpe had been dating, causing a massive fight, ending with Jasmine not speaking to Dylan for months on end. Dylan had spent his nights in warm beds, trying to hide from the fact that he missed his sister.

There were, at that time, certain aristocratic members of English society that were aware of vampires, young men and women who gladly shared a vein with the barest hint of a promise that one day, should they please a vampire, they might just be given immortal life.

It had been Adela who had approached him, dressed in her Victorian era dress, her corset making her breasts the focus point. Her long brunette hair was curled in to drape down her bared chest and when she placed a delicate hand on his arm, Dylan knew that it would take no words at all to hoist up her skirts and fuck her senseless.

Adela had smiled at him, sipping her red wine and licking her lips. It hadn't bothered Dylan that twenty minutes earlier, she had attempted to draw Malakai's attention, he just wanted to not think, not feel, and Adela bared her emotions as willingly as she bared her skin to him.

They had fucked in the coatroom, Adela laid flat on a bench as Dylan thrust in and out of her, using his power to know what the woman wanted and Dylan sated himself on her, sinking his fangs into her creamy skin as she took everything he offered and still she craved more.

Dylan kept going back to her, in the deep of night when her elderly husband slept. When he went away on business, Dylan treated the stately home like he was lord of the manor. He thought that he was in love with Adela, because why else would he continue to go back to her, night after night.

He indulged Adela's every whim. When he arrived one night to find her in bed with another man, her desire for him to join them, for him to have the man and her, Dylan fooled himself that it was his desire and not Adela's.

For about six months, Dylan didn't know where his feelings ended and Adela's began. It started to mess with his head and she knew it. She started to ask when he would make her a vampire, that she wanted to remain in her twenties as an immortal. Adela told him she loved him, wanted to be with him forever.

And Dylan had believed her, idiot that he was.

It was only when he arrived one night that he wasn't supposed to, and Adela was in bed with her other lover, the one she had persuaded Dylan to fuck, and Dylan heard Adela tell her lover that once Dylan made her a vampire, once she was immortal, she would turn him and then she would have no need for Dylan anymore.

It was in that moment Dylan felt her true emotions, not the fake love she pretended to have for Dylan. They were still in the throes of passion when Dylan had sauntered into the room enraged, at himself and Adela, who screamed as Dylan bared his fangs and ripped out her lover's throat while he was still inside Adela.

Dylan then turned his focus on Adela, listening amused as she proclaimed her love for Dylan, telling him that the tryst meant nothing and that she only called him to her bed because she missed Dylan. Not wanting to hear anymore, Dylan had dragged her by her hair out of the bed, telling her it was not a gift to became a vampire, it was a curse.

Dylan had then pierced her flesh, drinking her blood until her heart slowed, then stopped beating altogether. Then he tossed her body back on the bed beside her lover and walked out of the house.

It was one of his biggest regrets, letting his emotions get the better of him by killing Adela because he had felt like a fool. Deep down he had known all along, and he had killed Adela not because she had made a fool out of him, but because that was what Dylan had done to himself.

He had spent a lot of time after just hooking up with random Inferna and humans, men and women, not letting his heart factor in at all. It was a feeding of his body, like when he had to drink human blood. It might be a clinical way to look at it, but alas, it had been the truth for a long time.

However, when he was alone with Callista, he had no feelings from her to use as his own. It was just him, just how he felt, and his chest ached at the thought of being separated from her. He wanted Callista so badly that it gnawed at him like a hunger. But it was more than the sex, he craved the intimacy.

He wanted to be able to hold her hand in public, to kiss her freely. He wanted days in bed watching Catfish and giving her chocolates. He wanted to show her the world, as terrible as it could be, but remind her there was beauty in the terrible things as well as the breath-taking.

He was in love with Callista and for the first time in his life, Dylan wasn't terrified by his own feelings.

Dylan heard the bathroom door open and he pivoted around so he faced away from Callista. "Hey, I made you something to eat so you can have that before we rest for the day."

Callista didn't answer him, so Dylan rambled on. "It's just a bit of pasta and whatever I could find but if you don't want to eat that, then have a root through the fridge and I'm sure you can find something."

"Dylan."

The low tone as Callista uttered his name made him turn around. Her face was determined, it was the only word for it, but her eyes, those luminous green eyes held a hint of uncertainty. Her hair was braided to the side exposing the right side of her neck, like she knew that was the side of the neck he preferred to bite and he almost groaned remembering how good her body had felt against his.

She wore her leggings and vest, her feet bare as Dylan watched her swallow hard, striding down the steps and standing in the middle of the room, her next words would have certainly halted his heart if it still beat.

"I would like to call in my favour."

CHAPTER SEVENTEEN

Callista

"I WOULD LIKE TO CALL IN MY FAVOUR."

It had taken all her courage to walk out of the bathroom, her heart galloping like a horse ready to bolt. It was the stupid seer's fault, really, for she had been the one to whisper in her ear and told her to use the day to find out if the one Inferna she might like to rut with was Dylan.

Not that the thought had not crossed her mind on more than one occasion. The kisses they had shared had fogged her mind, her limbs becoming loose and a throbbing between her legs. It made her have rather inappropriate thoughts at inappropriate times.

Like when Dylan had gone to get her food, and Callista was remembering how tight the globes of his buttocks had been as he walked naked to his room, wanting to feel them with her hands, the Primus had stifled a laugh with a cough and Callista had felt embarrassed.

But the Primus had simply smiled at her, saying nothing as Dylan returned to the table with her chocolate and crisps. Her thoughts had been a jumble, not used to being in a room with Inferna who clearly cared deeply for one another. She had watched the interactions, up close now instead of at a distance. The easy way the Primus touched his fiancé and she him. The way the wolf just hauled his more than capable and strong mate into his arms when he felt her pain.

As a child, her mother tried to suppress her emotions. Dante had told her to embrace them, and then Vindicta, he had forced her to shatter them, so Callista could understand that now that the magic was failing on the tattoo, her emotions now were confusing. She knew how Dante had made her feel when she was a mere child, and perhaps she loved him, but it was like a child loves a parent.

But the vampire... there was this almost piercing pain at the thought of leaving him. Was that love? She did not know for certain. And yet, she wanted to do as the seer had advised and see if Dylan was the one Inferna she would like to make a mess with.

Perhaps her intentions were not obvious, for Callista had no skills in seduction, was not as adept as the vampire was and it made her feel silly, stupid. Dylan set the food he had prepared for her on the counter, striding around and down to stand on the other side of the couch.

She watched as he breathed in through his nose, nostrils flaring, no doubt scenting her arousal. Callista tried to not let her nervousness show on her face as she repeated. "I would like to call in my favour."

It was her safety net, the favour, just in case Dylan had not wanted to rut with her. Though from the bulge in his trousers and the heat in his eyes when he looked at her, Callista did not think she needed to use her favour for him to get naked with her.

And yet, she was a novice, the only rutting she had seen was the grunted fast couplings of the harpies, and even though she had watched Dylan kissing and making other men and women moan with pleasure, Callista had not stayed long enough to see how it ended.

"Strange time to call in your favour, Blue. Hit me with it."

Dylan braced his palms on the back of the couch as Callista worried at her bottom lip, acutely aware that the vampire tracked the movement like a predator did its prey. Wetness pooled at her core and Callista pressed her thighs tightly together, the ache almost unbearable.

"I want..." Callista cleared her throat, taking a moment before she tried again. "I want you to rut with me."

A slow seductive smile that Callista could only describe as smug curved his lips, but he stayed where he was, saying nothing. Callista crossed her arms and stripped off her vest, dropping it to the floor. "I want you to fuck me, vampire."

His open palms curled as Dylan grabbed the back of the couch, his lips parting, and his blue-green eyes were ablaze. It made her feel powerful, it made Callista feel like she was wanted.

Thinking back on the ruttings she had witnessed, Callista walked over to the opposite end of the couch, put her hands on the back, much like Dylan and spread her legs wide. A growl vibrated out of the vampire's throat as Callista's heart felt like it wanted out of her chest.

"What are you doing, Blue?" Dylan asked her, his voice lower than she had ever heard him speak.

"This is how you rut, right? I have seen other harpies fornicate like this. I have seen you rut like this. Am I presenting myself wrong?"

Callista was starting to babble, straightening and already regretting this absolutely hideous idea of being the one to try and seduce the vampire. Her cheeks heating, Callista made to go and grab her vest when Dylan moved.

A cool hand clasped the back of her neck, another rested on her hip as Dylan leaned in to her ear. "Oh, ya, I definitely want to take you from behind, watching as I drive you crazy and you tear at the furniture with those wicked talons of yours. I want you so hungry for my cock that you push that tight ass of yours back, telling me just how fast you want me to take you."

Dearest gods of Olympus.

Her body trembled in anticipation, a dark chuckle coming from the vampire. "Ya, Blue. I think you like that idea. Have you been thinking about that for a while? Has it invaded your thoughts like you've invaded mine?"

Callista nodded dumbly, was rewarded for her honestly as Dylan caressed her body, moving the hand at her hip along to her stomach, pulling her even closer, the hardness of his erection pressed against her back. Then Dylan continued to rub his hand upward, cupping her breast and Callista threw back her head, shocked at the heady moan that flowed from her lips.

"That's it, Blue. Let me hear how much you want me."

Dylan shifted his hand to fully cover her breast through her sports top, his fingers pinching her nipple and Callista hissed, her talons out now and then she heard Dylan groan in her ear, and she realized she must have moved her hands, as her talons now dug into his thighs.

"Jesus, Blue. That feels so fucking good."

His lips felt surprisingly warm against her skin or maybe she was just overheating at all the new sensations that were short-circuiting her mind. Dylan continued to blaze a trail along her throat, her shoulder, slipping the strap of her top down a little so that he could press an open mouth wet kiss to her shoulder, sucking the skin so hard there was no doubt it would leave a mark.

The throbbing between her legs seemed to increase and Callista needed to do something, anything to ease it, but she did not know how one could put a stop to the inferno building inside her. She wriggled against Dylan as his hand moved to her other breast and he pushed down the cup to cover her bare breast with his hand.

"Is this all part of the rutting?" she asked breathlessly.

"This is only the beginning, Blue." Dylan massaged her

breasts and her limbs felt like liquid. "There's a lot more mess to come before I finally get inside you."

Dearest gods of Olympus her core ached and she moaned, the vampire's lips now traveling along her jaw. Her core clenched, burning, begging her for release and she whimpered, embarrassed at how needy she sounded.

"I know what you want, Blue, but you need to tell me. I want to hear you say it out loud."

It seemed brazen, wanton to vocalize what was happening to her, and yet, Callista knew that Dylan would not ridicule her, he would not chide her or tell her what she was feeling was wrong.

"There is an ache and I do not know how to ease it."

A growl of satisfaction rumbled Dylan's chest against her back. "Tell me where you ache, love. Tell me where you ache."

Dylan pinched her nipple hard and she cried out. "Between my legs. Where the rutting happens. It hurts."

A wicked chuckle sounded in her ear. "Then touch yourself for me, Callista. Slip your hand into your shorts and slide a finger into your folds. Tell me if you are wet as you smell."

"Do you not...do you not want to touch me there yourself?" She asked, surprised when he nipped at her jaw.

"Oh, I will. But first I want you to know yourself, know what you want."

Callista shuddered at the directness, the pure lust in his tone as she slid her hand into her pants, into her briefs and along the slick wetness. She did not understand the way her body thrummed under her own fingers, wetness coating her fingers and she released a shaky breath.

"Well, Blue. Are you as wet as you smell?"

Withdrawing her hand, Callista looked at her damp fingers, not as disgusted by the mess as she considered she might be. Dylan took her wrist, lifting her fingers as he lowered his mouth, sucking her wetness off her fingers and she gasped, her legs threatening to go out from under her.

Greedily licking at her fingers, the vampire moaned, lifting his eyes to hers and Callista saw her downfall in his gaze. "You taste delicious, Blue."

Callista pulled back her hand, earning another dark laugh as she ground out. "That does not help the aching. My breasts are tingling, between my legs feels like I am burning up. I want to get to the rutting. I need your cock inside me now so that the aching may stop."

Dylan spun her round, taking her face in his hands, then their lips were crashing together, kissing, tasting, biting, then he lifted her so that she balanced on the back of the couch and Callista instinctively wrapped her legs around his hips, her heels digging into his buttocks, all sense leaving her the moment she felt his hardened shaft at the junction where she wanted it to be, only their clothing a barrier between them.

The vampire's arm went around her waist to hold her in place as Callista broke the kiss to claw at his t-shirt, dragging it up over Dylan's head and then she leaned in and kissed his chest, licking at his nipple as she roamed her hands over his body.

She learned the curve of his muscles, felt his stomach bunch under her fingers. She figured out that he liked a little pain as much as he liked to be petted, especially when she ran a talon over his nipple by mistake, and he sucked in a breath, so Callista did it again.

Dylan tore her sports bra off, then palmed her breasts, claiming her mouth again and again until Callista was arching into his groin, trying to find a way to soothe the ache in her core. As if he felt the urgency growing in her, Dylan slid his hands down to the curve of her buttocks, lifting her with ease and Callista flung her arms around his neck to hold on as he walked them to the bedroom.

He tossed her on the bed after another blistering kiss and

Callista bounced, a chortle of laughter escaping her that seemed to halt Dylan's advance. He looked at her like he had not seen her before as Callista leaned on her elbows and studied him.

"That sound. It's got to be the most beautiful melody I've ever heard in all my life."

Callista must have looked confused because Dylan kicked off his boots, crawling up the bed and hovered over her, dropping a kiss to her lips before he told her what he was referring to.

"The sound of your laughter. It is better than any song I've ever heard, any instrument I've heard played. I would spend my entire life trying to hear it again. I would give anything."

Her heart felt like it was about to explode and though Callista was still a little confused, trying to remember the last time she had laughed, and could not, it dawned on her that was what Dylan thought was the most beautiful sound he had ever heard.

She was a harpy who was not supposed to feel and he had made her laugh.

Desperately Callista grabbed for him, pulling Dylan down for another kiss. Callista did not have the fancy words or smoothness of the vampire taunting her, so she poured all of her feelings into the kiss, hoping that Dylan would know how much she craved him too.

Her chest was heaving when Dylan broke the kiss, as if he knew that she had forgotten she needed to breathe. He brushed the hair away from her face, tracing the talon mark on each of her eyes, then kissed them gently.

This was all taking far longer than she expected. It was not that she did not enjoy touching the vampire, because she did, but this was not what she had been expecting when she had decided to just get naked with Dylan. For one thing, they both still had their pants on and despite not knowing much about rutting, she did know that they needed to be naked for the rutting to happen.

Her core clenched and she wriggled uncomfortably beneath Dylan and her vampire looked down at her, clearly pleased with himself. She snarled at him, which only seemed to delight him even more and Callista wanted to punch him.

"Are you having fun so far, Blue? I know I am."

She smacked his arm, with a not so fierce growl. "This is not rutting. We are still dressed and I feel like I am going to go insane. You seem to delight in making me suffer."

"If kissing you and touching you and teasing you is driving you insane then I am doing my very best work. And there will be no rutting."

Callista must have looked absolutely horrified because Dylan barked out a laugh, shaking his head. "Who would have thought my harpy was this hungry for sex."

It occurred to Callista that Dylan might be mocking her, and she tried to roll out from underneath him, but he snatched her wrists and held her in place.

"We won't be rutting tonight," he started to explain, dropping kisses to her skin as he continued. "We won't be fucking. Oh, there will be, once we have more time, once you get as addicted to me as I am to you, Blue. I like having you in my bed and I want to keep you here, with me. I'm going to make love to you, slowly, maddingly so."

Dylan let go of her wrists and kissed his way down her torso, his hand roaming down to her hips, then curving under her buttocks, Callista lifting off the bed so Dylan could ease her leggings down her thighs and pull them off, then her shorts, throwing them aside as he spread her legs apart and licked his lips.

"Beautiful. I can't decide if I want to please you with my tongue or my fingers. I think I'll save the former for dessert. Right now, my cock feels like it's gonna break if I don't get inside you soon."

Callista leaned up more on her elbows, wanting to see what Dylan had planned for her and she watched as he bent her knees, sliding his hands up her thighs, one hand holding her hip firm against the bed, the other, oh the other brushed against the spot where Callista had touched herself before and her body jerked, with the vampire sliding a finger inside her.

She did not understand what Dylan intended to do to her now that his finger was inside her, then he flashed her a sinful smile and started to move his finger in and out of her. Callista slammed her hands onto the bed, her talons digging into the sheet and she let loose a long moan, a pressure building in her body, her head falling back, as she writhed underneath him, his finger powerfully stroking her to madness and when he added a second finger, she cursed, the pressure halting her breath and it was like the world stopped for one powerful thrust of his fingers, his thumb pressing down hard as Dylan all but purred. "That's it, Blue. Come for me."

It felt like an explosion, her body thrashing against the faster way his fingers delved into her. She cried out, her head going from side to side, her vision almost blanked as she vaguely heard Dylan muttering to her as he petted her mound and kissed her skin.

When she was able to think with some semblance of clarity, Callista turned her head to gaze at Dylan, her heart feeling like it had been opened for the first time in her life. The apprehension in his eyes made Callista want to take it away as she wiped the sweat from her brow.

"I have decided that I like the mess. I would very much like to make the mess again."

Dylan threw back his head and laughed and Callista smiled, knowing that her vampire, and he was hers now as much as she was his, Callista had decided, was utterly wrong when he told her that her laughter was the most beautiful sound in the world, because his laughter felt like the ocean against her skin.

Dropping a hard press of lips against hers, Dylan backed off the bed and never broke eye contact with her as he popped the button on his pants, an even hungrier glint in his eyes.

"We've only just started making a mess, Blue. We've only just started."

CHAPTER EIGHTEEN

Dylan

THE HUSKY LAUGH THAT TUMBLED FROM CALLISTA'S LIPS FELT like a caress on his skin. Dylan could never have imagined that the frosty harpy could hold within her the capacity for joy, but here she was, holding his gaze with a smile that made his chest ache.

The words that he had spoken to her, when he had told her that there would be no rutting, no fucking, had been the unblemished truth. During his lifetime, Dylan had been with a lot of partners, Callista knew and seemed to accept that, however, he had never made love to someone he cared for as much as Callista. It had pained him when she had arched her ass and asked him if she was presenting herself wrong.

And hell yeah, Dylan wanted to take her from behind, wanted to enjoy a quick hard fuck when she was ready. However, this was her first time, and it was a gift to him that she had after all these centuries of pretending to be heartless, that she would trust him enough to share this with him.

Dylan unbuttoned his pants, then slid the zipper down slowly, never breaking eye contact with Callista. His harpy was sensational, naked in his bed, her pale skin seemed ethereal, her blue hair falling over her breasts as she leaned up higher in the bed to watch him strip, her lips parted slightly, her lips kiss-swollen.

He had never felt so wanted. Dylan had never felt like he

was craved with the way Callista devoured him with her eyes.

Yanking off his pants, Dylan kicked them aside, then slowly, seductively, rolled down his boxers, taking his cock in his hands and groaning, as he watched Callista swallow, her eyes flaring while she tilted her head to the side.

"I did not realize it would be so big. I do not think it will fit inside me like your fingers did."

Her words were said with the barest hint of uncertainty, yet all Dylan could do was grin so hard his face hurt. "Oh it will fit. It will fit and feel way better than my fingers. But it does a vampire's ego good to hear you compliment the size of his cock."

Callista rolled her eyes, and just like that the uncertainty vanished. Dylan stroked his cock, his hand sliding up and down, Callista's eyes tracking the movement. Wetting her lips with a flick of her tongue, her breathing quickened, and when Dylan listened hard, he could almost, almost hear her heartbeat.

"I would like to use my hands on it. Your cock. Then I think I might like to see if it is as enjoyable as it looked when you put it in someone's mouth. I would very much like to lick it like a lollipop."

Dylan's cock jerked in his hand and his chest vibrated with a low growl. "Fuck, Blue. Just fuck. When this is all over, you and me are gonna spend days, no weeks, locked in a room where you can tell me all the little fantasies you want to fulfil. I will make it my life's mission to make sure you do."

That earned him another sexy-as-sin smile that pushed the blood in his veins to his heart and it fluttered. But Dylan didn't think it was entirely the blood. For centuries, Dylan had been dying slowly, each day more torturous than the last. Even more so when all his family seemed to be finding the person designed solely for them and them alone. He never dreamed of finding his mate, finding a person he could love like no other. But here she was, and he would fight to the death to keep her.

Dylan climbed atop the bed, crawling up from the end to where Callista waited for him. He claimed her mouth clasping his hands on the side of her face, taking his time to explore her mouth, lapping his tongue against hers, biting down on her bottom lip, encouraged when she reciprocated.

He took the time to work her up, arching his hips forward so that his length rubbed against her wet folds, repeating the action as he kissed her, until they were both groaning, until they were both panting, and until they were both on the edge of release.

With his hand under her head, Dylan lay her down on the bed, fanning her hair out so that he had a clear view of her face. He let his hands roam over her body, enjoying just how receptive to his touch she was and it struck him then that for the first time, he was only working on his instincts here, that he had not been able to use his power to deduce what a partner liked and Callista was wet and ready for him because she had liked everything Dylan had been doing to her.

He couldn't manipulate or be absolutely certain of Callista's feelings and it felt like freedom. Being with her, knowing that his power would not interfere in their relation-ship made Dylan smile.

Leaning down, Dylan rested his forehead against Callista's. "I'm going to make love to you now, Blue. It will hurt. If my magic worked on you, I would take the pain away and make it so that you only feel pleasure. I would never will-ingly hurt you."

Callista reached out with a hand, cupped his cheek. "I do not wish to ease the pain if there is any. I would like to feel it all. To know that it is real. I have been pretending not to feel for so long that I do not wish to pretend with you. I want to remember every single feeling I have this night."

In case we all die tomorrow.

Callista didn't have to say the words for Dylan to hear them, choosing to push the thought to the back of his mind so that he could be present in the moment. He roamed his hand up her sternum, faltering when his fingers grazed the tattoo and when Dylan placed his palm over it, he felt the rapid beat of her heart and it was a wonderous sound.

Dylan kissed her slowly, settling between her legs, his hardness poised at her entrance. He halted, checking that Callista was still all in with him and she nodded her head to his silent question. Dylan pushed in a little, felt her body tense under him, around his cock.

He pulled out, then edged back into her, repeating the action over and over while she adjusted to the brand new sensation, to the fullness of him. Dylan slid in a little further, felt Callista hiss and jerk, her hand clasping his shoulders as he pushed in a little more and more until he was fully inside her and he waited.

"Are you okay?" Dylan asked her, his words coming out like a grunt, relieved when Callista nodded, though she kept her hands gripped on his arms.

"Is it over?"

Dylan flashed her a grin. "The pain is over, Blue. Now comes that fun part where I make you lose control and scream my name."

Not giving her a chance to protest, Dylan reached between their joined bodies, rubbing her clit with his thumb and she relaxed beneath him. Dylan started moving slowly, pulling almost all the way out before sliding back in to the hilt, his other hand gripped her hip as he continued to make love to her, holding back the urge to go faster, harder, to claim her and taste her.

He kept the slow pace as Callista let loose a heady moan, started arching into his thrusts, and he increased the pace just a little as his harpy started to run her hands over his body. He removed his hand from between their bodies, reaching up to cup Callista's breast as he leaned his head down and took the other into his mouth and sucked, hard.

Callista bucked under him, making Dylan thrust into her harder than he intended and he froze, frightened he might have hurt her. His harpy was breathing hard as she locked eyes with him.

"Do that again. I would like you to do that again."

Jesus, Callista was perfect …she was just fucking perfect for him.

Dylan eased out of her body, heard Callista whimper and protest, then he slid back in harder and faster and she melted underneath him. She uttered his name and Dylan waited, needing to know she was still okay.

To punctuate her readiness, Callista grabbed his ass and tried to force his hips to move, causing Dylan to laugh darkly, until he felt the prick of her talons digging into his skin and his control snapped.

Dylan drove into her harder and faster, encouraged by the satisfied moan from his harpy, his balls slapping against her skin. His body felt like it was aflame, his skin tight and sweat began to trickle down his spine.

"Oh, Oh, I think…I feel like I might …."

Callista came hard, writhing against the sheets, tremors racking her body as Dylan kept up the pace, his own release almost upon him. He kept up his rhythm, felt his fangs ache in his gums before there was no way in hell that he could keep them sheathed. He was driven by a need to mark her.

Her orgasm subsided, her eyes blinking so she could focus on him as he started to shake himself because he was trying not to frighten her if he struck and bit her neck.

"Fuck, Callie, Blue. I need… bloody hell."

Callista removed her talons from his ass and stroked up his body. "What do you need?" She asked, almost breathless, nothing but a whisper.

"I need to bite you." He said, stilling for a moment. "I need to taste you."

Her response was simple. Callista angled her head to the side, exposing the slender curve of her neck and Dylan snarled, starting to move again, waiting until Callista was on the verge of another orgasm before he struck, latching onto her neck, his fangs piercing her skin, her blood filling his mouth.

Callista cried out his name as Dylan's release rushed ahead, and the next time he swallowed Callista's blood, he came, hard, his body rigid as he tore his mouth from her neck, careful to lick the wound closed and kissed Callista until she had wrung him dry and he felt undone.

Dylan braced himself over Callista, still buried deep inside her, afraid to move in case it broke the spell. Her eyes were closed, her chest heaving and then she opened her eyes.

"I would very much like to do that with you again."

Letting loose a bark of laughter that eased any tension in him, Dylan slowly pulled out of Callista, both of them groaning a little as Dylan leaned in to kiss her again. He would never tire of kissing her. He let her lay there for a few seconds, then he slid off the bed, going into the bathroom and returning with a washcloth.

He cleaned the space between her legs, making sure to take care of her before he slipped into the bed and pulled Callista into his arms. She rested her head on his chest, Dylan playing with the strands of her hair. It felt important, holding her like this. Like it might be the first and last time all rolled into one.

Dylan kissed the top of Callista's head, the harpy curling more into him, draping a leg over his and she sighed. "This is what people do after they ru- after they make love, is it not?"

He grinned to himself that she had changed the word rutting to make love, like Callista was learning the difference and it made him feel a very smug male satisfaction that it was because of him.

"I think so." Dylan admitted, continuing to stroke her hair. "I've not lingered in bed before to enjoy the after. I'm glad I get to do it with you though. I hope we get to have days where we just stay in bed all day and I get to have you in my arms."

"I think I would like that as well."

Callista became quiet after that, her breathing changing as she drifted off to sleep but Dylan found that he couldn't shut off his mind enough to rest. He closed his eyes, breathing in the scent of his harpy, hoping it would calm him, and yet, he lay awake for hours.

Dylan tried to figure out a way that would mean they succeeded. If what Callista said was true and Dante was trapped in his body, watching the horror Vindicta was inflicting, then was he worth trying to save? Callista would be devastated surely if they killed Vindicta and Dante. This was so far beyond anything that Dylan had lived through.

The Inferna were essentially beings created from Hell. They all carried a little bit of monster in them, whether you were fae, vampire, banshee, or harpy. They wandered the world consumed by humans, lingering in the shadows. Most religions and histories offered some sort of indication of the end of days, like the Norse tale of Ragnarök, but this was different because this was real life and there was a very big chance that if Vindicta opened a gate to hell, then death was a given for millions of people around the world.

Dylan sighed, easing Callista off him so that he could get out of bed. He pulled on his boxers, quietly so as not to wake Callista and slipped from the room. He paced for a little while, going over the plan for tonight in his head. It struck him that he could find the pages Zeke had given Callista, go back to Dante – Vindicta, all while Callista slept. She might never forgive him but it would keep her safe.

He was fooling himself if he thought she would stay with him if he pulled that stunt, because Callista was not in need of protection like Scarlett was. Dylan had fallen for the heart of a warrior, much like Kai had with Keeva.

Sitting down on the edge of the couch, Dylan closed his eyes.

How the hell do you stand it knowing you are about to send Keeva into danger?

Dylan sent the errant thought out to Malakai, hoping his brother wasn't in a compromising position right now or things would get real awkward, real fast.

You'll get used to the absolute helplessness of your mate running into danger.

Dylan heard both the amusement and the truth in Malakai's thought.

I think you're enjoying my suffering a little too much, brother.

Never that, Dylan. Never that. I have watched you suffer for centuries and it hurt me every time you slipped into a depression. I worried every time you disappeared for weeks with no word. It makes it easier not to worry that you have someone to come home to.

Dylan scrubbed his hand down his face.

I would always come back, Kai. I would never have let you worry too long.

Sighing, Dylan asked the next question.

Has Zeke changed his mind about Callista?

Silence filled his mind and Dylan could almost picture Malakai frowning, searching for the most diplomatic words to say everything he needed to say while not saying anything at all. If Dylan wasn't so torn, feeling like he was being pulled away from the woman he loved because his family were not willing to forgive, he might just have laughed.

Ezekiel is a work in progress. He will come around. Get some rest, Dylan. The end of this will not come easy.

Malakai cut the contact, leaving Dylan to get to his feet, knowing that Malakai was right, the end of this would not come easy, but one way or another, they would finish this tonight.

Dylan went back into the bedroom, closing the door quietly and slipping back into the bed where Callista had curled into herself, her back facing away from him. He curved his body around hers, one arm under his head and the other resting on her stomach.

Callista sighed, then turned toward him, snuggling into him and Dylan just wrapped his arms around her. She tucked her head against his chest, where his heart used to beat and Dylan felt complete, whole. It was strange, how he used to avoid this type of intimacy with others, ever since Adela, but even that had felt forced, like he was an actor playing a part.

But being here, in Callista's arms, felt like the most natural thing in the world and he wanted to spend the rest of his days holding her like this, and never let her go.

"Your thinking is keeping me awake." Callista mumbled sleepily against his chest, causing Dylan to laugh.

"I'm sorry. Go back to sleep. I promise to think a little more quietly."

Callista pushed off his chest, frowning. "Are you not tired? Was the rutting not good enough to make you tired?"

Dylan brushed her hair from her face, kissing her lips lightly. "It was everything I wanted and more. I am tired, but just can't sleep. It's got nothing to do with you or how epic the sex was."

"Then perhaps we should try and make you tired enough to fall asleep."

Dylan had little choice but to laugh as Callista pushed him down on the bed, throwing her leg over him as she straddled his legs, reaching down to take his cock in her hand, his shaft hardening under her firm grip. Callista focused on his face, stroking him, her pace quickening when he arched his hips up. He wanted to throw his head back, just not as much as he wanted to watch Callista.

With her hand still on his cock, she used her free hand to delve inside herself, a gasp escaping her lips and then she was lifting her ass off his legs, going to her knees, positioning his cock at her entrance. Dylan grabbed her hips as she started to lower herself onto him, wriggling as she tried to take as much of him as possible into herself.

Dylan arched into her to help her along, Callista slapped a hand on his chest and gave him a feral smile. He had so many thoughts in his head, but the moment Callista started to ride him, all coherent thoughts fled and Dylan lay back and let himself be taken by his harpy.

CHAPTER NINETEEN

Dylan

DYLAN HAD FALLEN ASLEEP IN CALLISTA'S ARMS AND WHEN HE woke, she was already coming out of the shower, offering Dylan a coy smile as he rolled toward her, curling his finger so that she would lean in and let him kiss her lips.

"You should have woken me and we could have showered together." Dylan remarked, his lips curving into a smile that quickly faltered when he watched Callista frown.

"I was trying to wash your scent off my skin." It was said in such a cold, matter-of -fact kind of way that Dylan hadn't expected, her expression not giving much away.

Dylan flinched at the coldness in her tone, in the abruptness of her words and he couldn't mask his expression in time. He turned his head away to shield Callista from the emotions in his eyes, jumping when he felt her warm hand on his face as she turned him back to face her.

"I am sorry." Callista said, trying to soften her expression. "I had not meant for it to come out sounding so callous. I will try again." Her hands clasped his neck, as if she meant to hold him in place. "I woke up worried that Vindicta would scent you on my skin and it would make you a target. I fear you have gotten under my skin and it may be my undoing."

Well, now he felt like an ass for feeling hurt. Dylan got to his feet, and kissed her jaw. "It's okay. It didn't even dawn on me to be worried about carrying each other's scent. I think you scrambled my brains."

Callista laughed huskily, then shoved him toward the bathroom. Dylan quickly showered, then dressed in similar clothes that he had on yesterday. When he emerged, Callista must have had a similar idea because she had put back on the leggings that he had peeled off her earlier and the vest. Her blue hair was pulled off her face into a ponytail and she glanced up at him from the edge of the bed as he came toward her, noticing that his harpy wasn't wearing a bra.

Dylan really wanted to delay the inevitable, would have tried his luck. However, he was halted by Callista, her palm on his chest as she held him at bay. "We do not have time for whatever has your eyes all aflame."

He winked at her, got a roll of eyes in return as Callista slid off the bed and out of his reach. They finished dressing in relative silence, Dylan unable to stop himself from going to her and zipping up her hoodie, then helping her strap her sword to her spine. He watched as she opened one of his drawers and pulled out the pages of Lucifer's book and slipped them inside her jacket.

They stood there, looking at one another for what felt like hours, neither of them wanting to step out of the bedroom and back to their reality. Dylan wanted to say something profound, he wanted to offer some words that would convey just how much Callista meant to him. He could not burden her with talk of mates when they had the fight of their lives and he was not as good with words as Kai, so instead, Dylan placed his hands on Callista's face and gave her the truth.

"I love you."

Callista closed her eyes, inhaled, like she was trying to scent if his words rang true or not. For a torturous amount of time, she kept her eyes shut, her lips closed, and Dylan could only think about Malakai's warning.

"Callista may not return your feelings, Dylan. What was done to her...what Dante or Vindicta did to her, she might not have the ability to feel the same way as you do."

In that moment, where Dylan was prepared to accept that Callista might never reciprocate his love, her eyes fluttered open, and Dylan stilled as she offered him a sad smile.

This was it, the moment where his heart was shattered into a million little pieces and it would feel like karma. This was what he deserved for manipulating emotions and using them for his own gain. He would be ruined, after this. Destroyed. Never to recover.

And then, she spoke, her words like a symphony to his ears. "I think that I love you also."

Relief filled his body as he leaned in to claim a kiss, wanting to cement this moment with his lips, his body, and his soul. But the end of the world was bearing down on them and a kiss would have to do for now.

They left the bliss of the apartment shortly after, neither of them saying a word, though when Dylan reached for Callista's hand, she took it, entwining her fingers in his as they traipsed through the tunnels. It took a lot less time to get to the place they needed to go than Dylan would have liked but Callista turned to face him, her expression fierce.

"Once Vindicta has the pages, you must leave me and try and free Scarlett. I will keep him distracted until you have her to safety."

"Blue…" Dylan started, but Callista shook her head, frowning as she began to speak once again.

"No. You must. He cannot have the child. If she is not safe, if the succubus does not survive, then I can never make amends so that we can be together. The obscurum will never accept me. I would not have your heart at war with itself because it is divided. This is how it must be."

Callista told him that once she was inside the room, she could summon a key and Dylan would be able to get Scarlett out of the cage. That she would handle Vindicta and Dylan, not at all happy that she was willing to put herself in harm's way for him, could only nod in agreement because Callista knew Vindicta better than he did.

They kissed once more, then climbed up the ladder, a sickening feeling in the pit of Dylan's stomach as they ended up back where they had started. Dylan brushed his fingers against Callista's, then they strode side by side back into the room, with Dylan immediately looking for Scarlett.

The succubus was sitting at the farthest edge of the cage, her hand out through the bars and her fingers clenched in the coarse hairs of the hellhound's neck. Tears filled her eyes when Scarlett spotted Dylan, as Callista went to pat her hound on the head.

"Are you okay?" Dylan asked Scarlett, striding round Callista and the hound to hug Scarlett through the bars after she slowly got to her feet.

"It's been a weird couple of days. I'll fill you in when we get out of here. Did you see Zeke? Did you see Keeva? Are they okay?"

Dylan kissed the back of her hand. "They tussled with Callista a little. Everyone's okay, I promise, but we need to get you out of here."

"Oh do not leave just yet. We have much to discuss."

Dylan snarled at the sound of Vindicta's voice, dropping Scarlett's hand so that he could stand in front of the succubus. A slow, smirk tipped the edges of Vindicta's lips as Dylan tried to remain calm and focused, not letting his anger cloud his judgement.

Vindicta stepped back as Ezra strode into the room, carrying a petite unconscious female who was bleeding quite heavily from a wound on her head. The werewolf looked like he wanted to be sick, guilt in his eyes as he set the unicorn down in the corner, not prepared when Dylan surged forward, smacking Ezra's head against the wall so hard Dylan heard bone crack.

The werewolf slid to the floor, knocked out but still

breathing. Roman would want to be the one to dole out his punishment, but Dylan felt happier that at least one threat was off the playing field.

Vindicta glanced at Ezra, shrugged when Dylan arched a brow, simply replying. "His incessant chatter bored me. You should have just killed him. I got what I needed from the unicorn."

"Ezra is not mine to deal with."

Dylan walked back over to the cage, trying hard not to glance at Callista to make sure she was okay, when Vindicta inhaled and then chortled with laughter. "So, you fucked him then? After centuries of waiting, was it worth it? Was the hard fuck worth it now that you can still feel him inside you?"

Not able to fight it anymore, Dylan turned to look at Callista, her face blank as she shrugged. "It was how I expected it to be. An itch to be scratched. Nothing more."

Vindicta was too busy laughing to notice the look they shared and had it not been for Scarlett resting a hand on his shoulder and jerking his gaze away, the heated exchange might have been caught by Vindicta.

"Give me the pages." Vindicta demanded, taking a menacing step toward Callista.

His harpy sighed, appearing bored by all of this as she reached into her jacket and withdrew the pages. Excitement rippled through Vindicta but Dylan could feel a hint of fear, and it made him consider if it was coming from Dante himself rather than Vindicta.

If Callista was right and Dante was trapped inside Vindicta, then Dylan wasn't entirely sure if he could kill Vindicta. Feeling his brother's emotions, even the slightest undercurrent, meant Dante might be able to come back from it all. If they could send the Prince of Hell back to where he came from.

Vindicta snatched the pages from Callista, his fingers gripping them tightly as he pulled out the book of Lucifer and turned away to slot the pages back into place. Callista summoned the key and tossed it at Dylan, who caught it and was already inserting it into the lock when a faint light started to glow from the book in Vindicta's hands. The light became brighter as Vindicta turned back around, his hand on the book as the words, the marks, shifted off the page and trailed along his skin, as if Vindicta was emptying the spells into himself.

Dylan wasted no time flinging open the door to the caged and beckoning Scarlett forward, surprised when the succubus hesitated, her hands on her bump. She shook her head when Dylan motioned for her to come to him.

"Oh the power. It is so much more. How does father stand it? All of the power of heaven and hell in his veins, unable to use it all. But I can. I can use it and create the world anew."

Vindicta was rambling, the glow of the book now fading to nothing. He tossed the book aside, ancient symbols marked on his skin and then, they glowed, causing Vindicta to grit his teeth and fall to one knee.

"Scarlet, come on. We need to get out of here."

Scarlett's entire body was shaking as she stepped out of the cage. Dylan doubled over from the force of her fear, causing him to groan and Scarlett lingered half in the cage and half out, trying to shield her feelings but the poor succubus was failing. Locking down his power as much as possible, he reached for Scarlett, just as Vindicta seemed to adjust to his newfound power and flung out a hand.

Dylan went sailing through the air, his shoulder hitting the wall hard enough to break bone. He didn't pause to let the bones heal, just lunged for Vindicta, screaming at Scarlett to run.

Vindicta stretched out his hand, his palm flat and Dylan froze mid-movement, suspended in motion unable to even twitch. Striding toward him, Vindicta's eyes glowed red, and Dylan knew he was going to die.

"I do not need you anymore, brother. You have served your purpose and are no longer useful."

Dylan shifted his gaze to Callista, wanting to convey his love for her but all he saw was a blur of movement, a blue streak in the darkened cell, as Callista bouldered into Vindicta, knocking him to the side and breaking the connection with Dylan. Callista whirled around, swinging her sword, aiming it right for Vindicta's neck. Dylan felt a wave of sadness as his harpy prepared herself to kill the vessel that held her mentor captive.

The blade halted a hairs breath from Vindicta's neck.

For the briefest of moments, Dylan thought Callista had fumbled, had decided she could not kill Vindicta because of Dante, and hope fled his bones. Then he heard her scream of frustration, knew it not to be true. Vindicta grinned, circling his finger in the air and Dylan watched as Callista's wrist bent in an inhuman way, causing her to drop the sword.

Torn between wanting to protect Scarlett and save Callista, Dylan stayed rooted to the spot as Vindicta reached out and placed a palm over the flesh where her heart was, where that goddamn tattoo was. Red light flared in Vindicta's palm and Callista screamed, her eyes darting to Dylan.

"Sneaky harpy. I should have known that the hold on you was slipping. You hid it well, my girl. But now? Now I know how to rip away your emotions completely, never to return. When I ask you to rip your mate's heart from his chest, you won't even feel a thing."

"Oh Dylan…"

Dylan heard Scarlett behind him, pain etched in his chest as he started forward, then was stopped by an outstretched palm from Vindicta.

"Dante, please. If you are still in there. Don't let him do this. I love her, brother. I love her."

Callista's scream sent a chill surging through him, and he yelled at Dante some more, all while Vindicta laughed and laughed. He stopped for a moment, turning his head so that he could watch Dylan's anguish, delight in his black and red eyes.

"Come on, Dante. Don't become the Prince's bitch. Show us just how powerful you are! Come on, Dante. Fight you son of a bitch."

Dylan had lost the feeble amount of hope he held on to as he could do nothing but watch the woman that he loved become what she feared. He could smell it now, all of her fear, and it brought tears to his eyes.

"Dante."

Power washed over him. Power he had only ever felt once before. Scarlett stepped out of the safety of her cage, the hellhound pressed firmly at her side, still obeying Callista's orders to protect the succubus. Saying Dante's name again with a little more impact and a muscle ticked in Vindicta's jaw.

Scarlett had only used this amount of power once before, when Zeke had gone full on ripper mode and she had called forth her power to subdue his hunger, exchanging the blood hunger for a hunger of another kind.

"Dante, you don't want to hurt Callista now, do you?" Her blue eyes seemed to glow, and Dylan felt his body harden under the brute force of Scarlett's power. Dylan wasn't sure, but this felt way more impactful than it had the last time, and he wondered if the baby was aiding Scarlett, their magic contained in one vessel for now.

Vindicta's hand snapped back from Callista, the harpy dropping to her knees in front of Vindicta, sucking in air as she clutched at her chest. She yanked her hoodie aside, relief flooding her face when she saw the tattoo had only darkened slightly.

Dylan dragged his gaze back to Vindicta, blinking in amazement at the brown eyes staring back at him. "Dylan. I can't hold him for long. Get out of here. Get them out of here."

Dante moaned, staggering backward and Dylan went to reach for his brother, his hand landing on his arm at the exact moment Vindicta retook control of Dante's body. Vindicta lashed out, striking Dylan hard in the chest, sending him crashing back against the cage, Scarlett ducking back inside to avoid behind hit.

Vindicta kicked him in the stomach, then again and again as he snarled, reaching down to drag Dylan up by the hair, pressing his head into the bars. "You think that your snivelling brother could stop me? He was so envious of you and your siblings that he welcomed me into himself without hesitation. He was never strong enough to withstand me and now, I have all of the knowledge in my veins to fulfil my plan. Your siblings I will make my own personal playthings. I will kill their mates. I have no use for you, vampire. Let me send you to hell so that you can suffer eternal damnation."

Vindicta yanked Dylan's head to the side, baring Dante's fangs as if he meant to rip Dylan's throat out and feast on his soul. Dylan closed his eyes, not wanting to see his brother's face in the moment of his own death. He heard a battle cry, his eyes darting open as Vindicta lost his grip on Dylan and Callista shrieked, her talons slashing at Vindicta's face and the Prince of Hell had to shield his face with his hands to stop Callista from tearing the flesh, her rage slashing at Vindicta's arms.

Copper scented the air as Callista managed to force Vindicta on his back, Dylan's harpy straddling his chest as she slashed and slashed, spilling blood and most definitely making a mess.

Callista looked every bit as terrifying as the infamous nature of her kin, her bloodlust almost tragic in just how beautiful it was, as she shrieked, continuing her assault on Vindicta, who seemed so taken aback by the violence from

Callista, that it seemed to make him forget about all the power brimming inside him. Flesh and blood splattered, on Callista, on the floor, on the walls as his beautiful harpy lifted her right hand, talons poised to rip out Vindicta's throat as she snarled and Dylan fell in love all over again.

"Do not dare touch my mate! I will fucking kill you."

Yeah, his mate was definitely a badass. Definitely a fucking badass.

CHAPTER TWENTY

Callista

BLOOD AND FLESH TORE UNDER THE BRUTE FORCE OF HER TALONS and Callista had a moment of panic as she considered that her own skin and clothing was now splattered with gore. Then she came to the realization that this viciousness was a part of her, the harpy in her, and there was no need to feel anxious or afraid of the blood she spilled, because Callista was trying to protect her mate.

Mate.

It was rare for harpies to find a mate because they lacked emotions and the bond between Inferna was tricky when one-sided, however, her heart belonged to Dylan, her body and soul too and she would unleash an endless amount of wrath to keep him safe.

Vindicta shoved a pulse of magic at her, sending her careening back and Callista rolled into a crouch, ready to go again. Getting to his feet, Vindicta muttered under his breath and the wounds Callista had inflicted vanished, as if her outburst had not even happened. Surprise must have shown on her face because Vindicta laughed, the sound so dark and twisted that Callista knew it could not have come from the man who had saved her all those centuries ago.

"It was a gallant effort, harpy. A gallant effort indeed. I'm not quite sure your Dante likes the fact you've claimed his brother as your mate. It matters little though, considering you'll both die this night."

Vindicta closed his eyes and Callista felt the rising power coming from the Prince of Hell and she leapt out of the way just as he sent a ball of flames toward her. Dylan started toward Vindicta, who gave a nonchalant wave of his hand and her vampire went flying across the room, and Callista heard more bones crack.

Callista ran to where Dylan was slumped, brushing the strands of blond hair that had come loose from around his face. He groaned in pain, lifting his hand to the back of his head and it came away bloody. "I'm okay. I'm okay."

His repetition of the words gave her little comfort as she got to her feet and looked over to Vindicta. Archaic words flared on his skin and then he turned toward Scarlett. "You have stirred something in me that I did not conceive ever feeling again. The power in you, I've felt it only once before. In Lilith." Vindicta seemed almost giddy at the prospect of the first seductress and Scarlett having the same powers. He took a step toward the cage, focused now on the succubus, as if he had dismissed her and Dylan as threats.

Reaching out with his hand, his palm turned up, Vindicta slowly curved his lips into a smile that could only be described as predatory. Lagertha snarled, drool hissing as it dropped from her mouth, the hellhound pressing closer to the bars. Vindicta did not even glance in Lagertha's direction.

"Take my hand. Take my hand and when I become a god, you will become a goddess. The Inferna who once ridiculed you will fall to their knees and worship you. I will even give the child to any of the Sicarius vampires that survive."

Scarlett shook her head back and forth. "The difference between you and me." She began, her voice shaky. "Is that I don't want the power. I want to have a family. I want to raise my daughter. And you forget, I already have a mate. I bet he's looking forward to tearing you to pieces."

Vindicta snickered, standing just outside the cage and Callista wondered if Vindicta's stolen power would also be nullified should he find himself inside the cage. The Prince was so focused on Scarlett that he did not see the threat coming down the darkened corridor.

Ezekiel Collins looked even more menacing as before, a vicious snarl curling his lips as he beheld Scarlett cowering in the cage. Vindicta had yet to even notice that the obscurum stood in the doorway, murderous intentions in his eyes.

Scarlett clasped a hand over her mouth as the obscurum moved, a dagger in his hand. He aimed for the back of Vindicta's neck, hoping to paralyse him for a moment and gain the upper hand. Moving at the last possible moment, Vindicta hissed as the blade went into his shoulder and he flashed from one spot to another away from the obscurum and closer to where Callista was still shielding Dylan.

Vindicta yanked the blade from his shoulder, and sniffed it before snorting and tossing it back to Ezekiel, who caught it with ease, even as the obscurum blocked his way to Scarlett. Ezekiel looked at his mate, his face softening. "Are you okay? Is Grayce okay?"

Scarlett's smile seemed to light up the room. "We are now. I love you."

"I love you too."

Vindicta clapped, a slow, exaggerated clap that had the hairs on the back of her neck standing to attention. "Well done. Well done indeed, Ezekiel. I don't know how you managed to find me but I applaud you. And your mate, you chose a mate who has within her the power of Lilith. If you were a man who craved power like Dante was, she would be the key. The blade was a nice touch though. How did you manage to find a holy blade touched by an angel?"

The obscurum kept his mouth shut, his almost black eyes focused only on Vindicta. Callista had been wondering also how the obscurum had been able to locate them, when the building, and Vindicta himself, were spelled to ward off any tracking.

As if he sensed her question, Dylan gingerly got to his feet and grazed his fingers against hers. Callista peered at him, her mate looking sheepish.

"I swallowed a tracker. Back at home. I'm sorry I didn't tell you but I wasn't sure if Vindicta could compel you to tell him. If Zeke is here, we should have backup."

It stung a little that Dylan had not trusted her with the truth, however, she did understand. Callista leaned into his shoulder, then went back to focusing on the staring match going on. The obscurum took a menacing step toward Vindicta, who in turn lifted his hand to try and stop Ezekiel's momentum, but the obscurum just seemed to brush it off.

Frustration made Vindicta growl, his fangs elongating as he reached out to the side and began to lift both his hands upward. The obscurum stopped walking, growling as he began to mumble a prayer and Callista could smell blood.

"Zeke! Down!"

The obscurum obeyed the order from the banshee, dropping to his stomach on the ground as Keeva stormed into the room, with what looked like a plastic toy shooter in her hands. She grinned at Scarlett, as Dylan barked out a laugh, Keeva holding the toy up and aiming it at Vindicta.

Vindicta's expression looked puzzled as he regarded Keeva, narrowing his gaze. The banshee might be petite but she had the fierceness of a warrior in her marrow. Although Callista did not understand what her next words meant at all.

"Say hello to my little friend."

Keeva pumped the toy a few times, then shot, water firing at Vindicta and Vindicta roared, at the exact moment that Dylan whooped and laughed. Vindicta's skin sizzled as Keeva continued to fire.

"Holy water. Holy fucking water in a super soaker! It's bloody genius" Dylan said, sounding proud of his future sister-in-law but Callista could smell the scent of burnt flesh and when Vindicta screamed, Callista could only see that Keeva was killing Dante, not just Vindicta.

Callista must have taken a step forward because Dylan grabbed her arm. "Is this how it ends? Must I lose him? Must I grieve for the man who raised me at a time I should be rejoicing that I found you? There must be another way. There must."

Dylan hugged her to him, yet he did not say a word, and Callista knew that he must mourn too, losing his brother twice in a lifetime. Keeva ran out of water as Vindicta went down on one knee, and she tossed the toy aside to look over her shoulder at them, and the obscurum started to get to his feet.

Callista untangled herself from Dylan and started to walk forward when she felt the ripple of anger and magic, shouted a warning as Vindicta clenched his fists and lifted his arms, only to punch the ground and send a pulse of magic toward them.

Callista grabbed hold of the bars of the cage, managing to keep herself upright as the rest of the Inferna in the room were thrown to the ground. Vindicta rose to his full height, eyes blazing red as he roared, a flicker of flames building in his grasp as he readied to fire it at the obscurum and the banshee, the later helping Keeva to her feet.

The fire would kill them both.

Callista bolted toward the path of the magical flames, the sound of Scarlett's scream and Dylan's cry of her name ringing in her ears. And then, she stopped, held in place by power of untold magnitude, unable to move even a finger in the slightest. Her heart pounded in her chest as she waited for the death blow to come.

And yet, it never did.

Callista came back into motion, only to be tackled to the ground by Dylan and when Callista lifted her eyes, she beheld the seer in all her glory.

Hair fanned out as if wind lifted it, her eyes were as black as Vindicta's, her legs parted and her hands held up in front of her. Vindicta was frozen, unable to move, as were the obscurum and the banshee. The entire room was frozen apart from Dylan and herself.

"How are you immune to her power?"

Dylan winked, kissing her hard on the mouth before he said. "Later, Blue. I'll tell ya later."

Helping her to her feet, Dylan pushed his friends out of the path of the flame as the seer grunted, her arms starting to tremble as she barked out a warning, and time started to move once more. Jasmine staggered, yelping as the fireball came toward her and she darted to the left moments before the fire would have hit her.

The room was not very large and the more Sicarius Inferna that came into the room made it so much smaller, with more chances for Vindicta's aim to hit true. Callista knew that it was vitally important to get Scarlett out of the room as quickly as possible. But Vindicta was standing in the path to the door, making escape impossible for now.

Vindicta shook out his limbs, smiling at Jasmine. "You just won't die, will you? How many times do I have to try and end you? You know, he struggled the most when I wanted to hurt you. Dante. I had to keep him at bay. No matter how envious he became of your brothers, he hated hurting you."

Jasmine let loose a sob and Vindicta did not even hesitate as he lashed out with his hand, aiming to separate Jasmine's head from her shoulders. Callista *moved*, faster than she had in her life, pushing Jasmine out of the path of the strike, the blow hitting her in the shoulder, causing Callista to spin and hit the wall hard.

Roman caught Jasmine as he entered the room, and Callista blew out a shaky breath as she tried to stand of her own accord, but had to brace a hand on the wall, pain lancing her shoulder. Dylan made to come forward, but

Callista was assessing the room, looking for a way to retreat.

Primus…can you hear me?

Callista could not be certain that Malakai was lingering somewhere outside and while she might not understand love and the bonds of family all that much, she had to assume that Malakai would not have let his mate venture off into danger when her death was forecast.

I can…what can I do for you, Callista?

Callista quickly explained her plan to Malakai, felt the approval in her mind of the plan, then watched as Malakai spoke into the minds of the Inferna in the room. Vindicta sniffed, rolling his eyes as he watched the exchange.

"Malakai, Malakai, Malakai. Always happy to let others fight your battles. Sending your mate in as the first line of defence. Cowardice. Why don't you and me settle this? It was always you Dante had issue with. The younger brother with the air of entitlement, the power wasted on you."

The Inferna by the door seemed to part, making the Primus' entrance seem much more dramatic, more staged. Malakai Cavanagh strode in wearing all black; black suit, black shirt, black shoes. If the devil himself had walked into a room, this is what Callista guessed he would look like. Malakai brushed down the front of his suit, flicked an imaginary piece of fluff from his jacket, then and only then did he bother to look at Vindicta.

"So, you are the demon causing all this fuss. I'll be honest. I was expecting more."

A muscle ticked in Vindicta's jaw, the only indication that Malakai was getting to him. Roman snuck over to where the unicorn still lay, gathered her in his arms and left the room. Jasmine dragged Ezra, seemingly enjoying pulling his unconscious body along the ground.

That took four Inferna from the room.

Malakai made a show of pacing around the room, like

there was no threat and he was simply surveying the room, but he was forcing Vindicta to move when he moved, allowing for the banshee to coax Scarlett from the cage, but Vindicta spotted them and whirled around ready to strike at Keeva.

Callista heard the ear-splitting howl as Lagertha bounded around the cage and lunged at Vindicta, catching the demon's arm in her massive jaws, whipping her head back and forth as Keeva scrambled, her arm around the succubus and then the obscurum glanced at Malakai who nodded.

Vindicta grabbed Lagertha by the scruff of the neck with his free hand and ripped her teeth from his flesh, the wound already starting to heal as he tossed the hound to the side and Callista screamed as her hound yelped once as she hit the wall and then lay in a crumbled heap on the ground. Tears pricked her eyes and Callista forced herself not to think that Lagertha might be dead. The obscurum and Malakai stalked Vindicta, with Malakai to his front and Ezekiel at his back, leaving him unable to protect himself from both angles.

"Dante was weak. A fool. He could never have stood up to me without you wearing his face. A mild inconvenience."

Vindicta growled, inching closer to Malakai, not realizing that would be his undoing.

Ezekiel rugby tackled Vindicta, catching Vindicta by surprise, dragging him sideways and into the spelled cage. The obscurum punched Vindicta, who tried to shield himself with magic, the shocked expression when he could not, making Callista laugh as she sagged, grateful for Dylan's arms as they wrapped around her waist from behind.

The obscurum kept hitting Vindicta, the demon bleeding profusely from his face as Malakai walked forward, putting his hand on the door of the cage. "Zeke, that is enough. He's not going anywhere."

The menacing obscurum in the cage brought his knee up, connecting with Vindicta's groin, then shoved the demon-possessed vampire to the ground as he strode out of the cage, yanking the door from Malakai's grasp and slamming it shut, with Vindicta caged inside.

Vindicta wiped blood from his lip and laughed, looking at Callista. "Do you really think they will let you live knowing that you made it possible for me to get to them? That it was your intel that made it all possible. I will get out of this cage, in time. But you'll already be dead. I wonder will they make your mate do it? Can I watch?"

Callista heard a whimper as the members of the Sicarius Security team all filtered back in, Lagertha shaking her head as she made her way toward Scarlett, her brimstone eyes looking at Callista, who nodded, understanding.

"You can call off the hellhound now. I'm okay." Scarlett said as she patted the hound on the head, Lagertha nudging her hand when the succubus stopped, causing her to laugh.

Callista shook her head. "She has bonded to you and your child. As it should be. She will protect you and your babe. Please look after her."

Scarlett burst into tears, allowing the obscurum to take her once more from the room. Dylan's hand went to Callista's hip, tightened, a growl rumbling in his chest as he looked at Malakai. "I can't let you hurt her."

The Primus simply stared at his brother, not a flicker of emotion in his gaze and Callista was about to step forward and tell them she was willing to take any punishment she deserved, in order to keep Dylan safe, when Jasmine sighed, stepping in between her two brothers.

"Well, Callie saved my life and it was her plan to trap Vindicta in the cage until we can figure out how to get the bastard out of Dante's body. I vote we keep her."

Dylan snorted, pulling Callista flush against him. She rolled her eyes, sighing, then looked at the Primus, who simply shrugged. "Looks like my vote doesn't matter."

Jasmine yanked Callista free of Dylan's grasp, pulling her

in for a hug. "Welcome to our weird and wonderful family, Callie. We can totally forgive you for trying to kill us. I mean, it's almost like an initiation, really. Keeva tried to kill Malakai, Zeke could have killed Scarlett, and I thought Roman would be the death of me. You'll fit right in!"

CHAPTER TWENTY-ONE

Dylan

"I DO NOT THINK THIS IS A GOOD IDEA."

Dylan kissed the nape of her neck, inhaling his mate's scent as she sighed her annoyance, though Dylan knew that she wasn't really annoyed at him, more anxious to be attending her first proper family gathering. Callista had voiced her fear that his family might never really forgive her for her involvement with Vindicta, even when Dylan told her that they understood her loyalty to Dante and her desire to protect him, not Vindicta. That didn't stop her from stressing as they rode the elevator up to where the party was happening,

They had spent a lot of time in his apartment for the same reason that Callista hadn't wanted to come today. When Dylan had asked her to move in with him, here to Sicarius, Callista had blanched and asked for time to consider his offer.

So, Dylan had been willing to give her some time, some space to get used to her new normal and to be fair, he was enjoying all the alone time with his mate. After securing Vindicta in the cells below Sicarius, moving the cage from Vindicta's lair to their homebase, they had left him in Malakai's custody and driven to the apartment where he had barely closed the door behind them before Callista had begun to rip his clothes off, pulling him down to the ground as Dylan gladly let her use his body.

It belonged to her now, along with his heart...his soul.

They had spent a few days in newly mated bliss, naked for the most part until a knock had sounded on his door and Dylan had opened it, not in the least surprised to see Jasmine standing at the door, brushing past Dylan and shouting for Callista, telling her to get her ass out of bed because they were going shopping.

Callista had looked horrified at the prospect of being alone with his sister, and venturing outside, but Jasmine had waved Dylan off and taken out her laptop. When Dylan had asked her about how she had known about his secret apartment, Jasmine had snorted, tapping the side of her head before she said. "I know everything, bro. Now let me and Callie shop."

He had left them to it, going to the bedroom to get some work done and after a few hours, when he emerged, it was like Jasmine and Callista had been friends all their lives. Before she had left, Dylan took Jasmine to the side and kissed her cheek.

"What was that for?" She had asked with a smile.

"For making her feel welcome. For understanding what she means to me."

Jasmine had shrugged her shoulders. "She's yours, Dylan. We love you so it means she's ours too. It's actually nice that we all have someone now."

Callista shifted in his grasp and fidgeted with the end of her shirt. It had been strange to see the clothes Jasmine had helped Callista pick out. Today she wore black leggings, a longline sleeveless t-shirt and one of his shirts, rolled up at the sleeves and her long blue hair was braided into a plait.

Dylan rested his chin on her shoulder. "It'll be grand. I promise."

Just over a week had passed since the confrontation with Vindicta but they were no closer to finding out how to remove Vindicta without killing Dante in the process. Zeke had been all for everyone leaving him alone in the cage with Vindicta, but no one else thought that to be a smart idea.

It had been a logistical nightmare trying to figure out how to get Vindicta, inside the cage, back to Sicarius without doing anything to mess with the magic that kept him contained. They had teams of agents guarding him, until Roman joked that they should just take the whole room and put it in the prison cells.

That had given Malakai the idea to cut the floor around the cage, hoist it out of the building and place it on the back of a truck in the dead of night. They had spent a day or two getting everything together, from Malakai using Sicarius funds to buy the building, pulling in all resources and a literal army marching beside the truck in case Vindicta managed to weasel his way out of it.

They had then wheeled him into one of the larger cells, removing all the bars first, replacing them with bulletproof glass that would only open on command from very few people in Sicarius. Vindicta had been quiet, too quiet, refusing to answer any questions he or Malakai asked him.

In the end, they had stopped asking, choosing to carry on with their own research rather than depend on Vindicta's cooperation. Neither had gotten them anywhere yet, but Dylan was hopeful.

Callista spun in his grasp, rubbing herself against him and he hissed through his teeth as she slid a hand between their bodies and cupped him through his jeans. "We could go back home and I could practice some more with your cock in my mouth."

Dylan speared his hands into her hair, kissing her with tongue and teeth as Callista continued to rub her hand up and down his jean-clad shaft, knowing it was driving him insane. The elevator doors opened as Dylan continued to devour her mouth, not caring that everyone in the family room could see them, Callista the one to break them apart when someone wolf-whistled.

Turning Callista round to face forward, making sure she

stood in front while he adjusted the erection in his pants and pulled his tee out of his jeans to cover it. Dylan gently pushed her forward, earning a glare for his troubles.

"It'll be grand." Dylan tried to reassure her, lifting his gaze to look at Malakai, who nodded. They'd had a long conversation last night, asking if both Scarlett and Zeke would be okay if he rocked up with Callista, with Malakai telling Dylan that he would speak to them.

While he wasn't opposed to another few weeks or months tangled up in bed with Callista, the sooner she got used to his family and they to her, the sooner he could start to look forward to the future.

They stepped off the elevator into an array of pink everything. Balloons and banners and bunting were all in a hideous shade of pink that hurt Dylan's eyes and it must have not been to Callista's liking either because he watched her scrunch her nose and mutter. "It is like something pink just exploded in here."

Dylan slipped his hand into hers, gave it a squeeze as they walked over to the table, where Malakai and Keeva were sitting, Keeva frowning at something Malakai said. They stopped talking when he and Callista came closer, with Keeva slumping back in her chair, her arms crossed defensively over her chest.

"Your brother's being an ass."

Dylan could feel her frustration as well as Malakai's but instead of trying to lessen it, Dylan let them wallow in it themselves as he shrugged. "You agreed to marry him."

"Ya, well, I might just rescind that agreement if he doesn't meet me at least half way."

Malakai looked aghast at Keeva's words, as she blew out breath. "You know I don't mean that but I don't want a massive, expensive wedding. We could get married here, right now and I'd be happy. You're already in a suit and I really would rather not wear one of those poofy monstrosities Jasmine picked out for me."

"Hey! I heard that!"

Keeva ignored Jasmine, motioning for Dylan and Callista to sit as she said. "Malakai seems to think we need a big wedding, where he has to invite every Inferna alive. I would much rather it just be family, an informal affair but he doesn't believe me."

Malakai shrugged, rubbing his temple. "Don't most girls dream of big weddings and a poofy dress?"

Dylan chuckled, mock punching Keeva in the shoulder. "Kai, you've met Keeva, right? She once refused a bed for the night when there was a bounty on her head because she didn't want to be under any obligation. If she wants a tiny wedding, then go with that or else you won't get to have the fun, just married sex."

Malakai considered Dylan's words, standing up so fast that his chair toppled over. "Then let's just get married. Right here, right now."

Keeva laughed, rolling her eyes. "I know we have the marriage licence and all but slow down, Kai. It's Scarlett and Zeke's day. Anyways, where the hell would you find someone to marry us at this short notice?"

Malakai looked crestfallen, clearly disappointed. Dylan heard Callista clear her throat. "The obs- Ezekiel was once almost a priest. Would it not be the same if he married you both?"

Callista was trying very hard to adjust to calling people by their names rather than titles or creature, so Dylan squeezed her hand in encouragement.

Keeva's eyes widened and she grinned. "That's fucking genius. Oh, my fucking god, married by the Monk. It's like ... the best wedding present ever. Do you think he would agree?"

The couple left him and Callista then, and Dylan lifted her

hand to kiss her knuckles. "That was nice of you to suggest Zeke. I don't think I would even have considered it."

Callista shrugged, but from the relaxedness of her shoulders, he could tell she was pleased to have contributed something. The tattoo was still etched on her skin, faded now to a grey, like a tattoo that had too much exposure to the sun. But it still masked most of her emotions from him, his powers all but useless on his harpy.

He would never be happy for the torture Vindicta had inflicted on Callista to smother her emotions, never. However, the fact that his power was null and void when it came to Callista meant he had to work extra hard to earn each smile, each and every peel of laughter, every kiss. He had to learn what made her sigh in frustration, what terrified her, what soothed her when she woke with nightmares, and what made her shudder in pleasure.

Dylan never realized how much he had relied on his power before, not until his Blue.

Malakai called his name, and Dylan made sure Callista would be okay before he got up and went over to help Malakai move some furniture. Jasmine whisked Keeva off into the back, much to Keeva's horror, as Roman and Zeke did something on a laptop.

Scarlett remained where she was, seated on the couch, and every time she tried to get up to help, Zeke grunted or growled. Scarlett flipped him off, causing them all to laugh, the hellhound curled up at Scarlett's feet lifting her head, smoke huffing out of Lagertha's nose before she went back to sleep.

When the room was suitably righted, Dylan stood in front of his older brother and righted his tie. "Last chance to back out, Kai. You sure you want to do this today?"

Malakai grinned back at him. "I was too up in my head about it all. I just want Keeva. She was never going to be happy with a big wedding. Family. That's all we need. And

I'd much rather call her my wife."

Zeke came toward them, a very serious expression on his face as he held up a printed certificate saying he had been ordained as a minister online. "Are you sure you wish for me to marry you, Malakai? We could always find someone more worthy."

Malakai clasped Zeke on the shoulder. "There is no one else we would rather have marry us. We should have thought of it sooner. Thankfully, Callista reminded us." Malakai grinned, flashing teeth. "Besides, I think Keeva is more excited that she can brag that the Monk married her, than she is about marrying me."

A steady stream of laughter erupted from Zeke's mouth, shaking his head as Jasmine emerged from the spare room and stepped aside. Keeva was dressed in a simple emerald green dress that clung to every curve she had, her curly red hair loose around her shoulders. Dylan grinned as he glanced down at Keeva's bare feet, his smile widening at the bouquet of flowers in her hand.

Keeva padded across the room, brimming with excitement and happiness, and it made him glance over his shoulder at Callista, who sat at the kitchen table, panic in her eyes as she wasn't sure what to do with herself.

"Callie! Come sit by me." Scarlett called out to his mate and Dylan could have kissed the succubus.

Callista walked over to the couch, sitting down stiffly beside Scarlett, who in turn linked her arm through Callista's. His harpy patted Scarlett on the arm, tears already in the succubus' eyes as she dapped her eyes. "I love weddings."

Zeke cleared his throat, beckoning Keeva and Malakai forward and Dylan stood beside his brother, while Jasmine stood next to Keeva.

"I'm only standing here because it would take Scarlett too long to get to her feet and she really shouldn't be standing.

Also, Zeke, I'd skip all the flowery lovey-dovey shit and get right to it."

Keeva burst out laughing, handing Jasmine her flowers so that Kai could take her hands.

"Okay, as Jazz so delicately put it, let's skip to the good part." Zeke announced with a grin, holding a hand over Malakai and Keeva's joined hands. "Keeva, do you take Malakai to be your husband?"

"Hell ya, I do."

Everyone laughed, except for Scarlett who was openly sobbing and muttering about hormones.

"Malakai," Zeke continued, taking his duties very seriously. "Do you take Keeva to be your wife?"

Malakai grinned, winking at Keeva as he said. "Hell ya, I do."

There was more laughter, as Dylan caught Jasmine's eyes going white, her grin telling him that nothing bad was going to happen, her quick remark to tell Zeke he needed to hurry up, drawing a snort of amusement from Dylan.

Looking over at Callista, Dylan felt a rush of love course through him. She returned his smile, still patting Scarlett's arm as the succubus winced, a jolt of pain hitting Dylan centre mass, as he glanced down to see if Callista's talons had come out but they hadn't.

Dylan reached out, taking some of Scarlett's pain, hitting him square in the gut and he barked out a curse. What the actual fuck?

"We really need to get a move on Zeke." Jasmine mumbled again, drawing a glare from Zeke, and Jasmine just shrugged.

"Fuck, we don't have rings." Zeke remarked, scratching his head but Jasmine just waved her hand, two rings seemed to magically appear in her hand.

"I got this all handled. Now hurry up!"

Keeva and Malakai exchanged rings, the simple bands

much more to Keeva's taste than Kai's but Dylan was sure that his brother would continue to try and shower his mate and now his wife, in diamonds. Because Dylan knew that to Malakai, Keeva was worth more than diamonds, worth more than any amount of money, and Dylan understood it now.

"By the power given to me by becomeaminster.ie, I now pronounce you husband and wife. Malakai, you may kiss your-"

Cheers and clapping, along with lots of laughter erupted as Malakai pulled Keeva to him, bending her backwards to kiss her like in one of those old-fashioned black and white movies. Jasmine threw confetti over the now-married couple.

Dylan felt a wave of sheer agony, and he clutched at his stomach, groaning, with everyone looking at him with wide eyes. The pain subsided, and he slowly straightened, shaking his head.

"It's not me...it's not me that's in pain."

Scarlett let loose a string of curses, shuffling forward in her seat as she clutched her stomach, and looked at Zeke in absolute terror. "I think," she ground out. "That Grayce didn't want to be left out of the wedding. I think my waters just broke."

Everything happened quickly from then on, with Zeke scoping Scarlett up in his arms, yelling for someone to call their midwife, heading down in the elevator to his and Scarlett's floor where they had planned to be when Scarlett gave birth. After feeling just how much pain Scarlett was in, Dylan had a newfound respect for the succubus.

Malakai and Keeva held off from consummating their marriage, Keeva anxious to make sure that Scarlett was okay and both mother and baby were healthy before they could leave. Dylan and Callista kept themselves busy making food and drinks, night turning quickly to day and still no sign of the baby.

Keeva, who had gotten frustrated a couple of hours in,

had returned pale as a vampire, her eyes filled with fear. "Keep Jasmine away from me, please. It does not look fun trying to push a tiny human out of your vagina. Nope. Not fun at all."

Malakai had simply smiled at Keeva, embracing his wife and pressing a kiss to her lips as Jasmine rolled her eyes, dismissing Keeva with a wave of her hand. "That's not what you say in a few years. We can talk then."

Joy...unbridled joy and laughter filled the space and Dylan absorbed it all, letting himself get drunk on it, the happiness he never dreamed could be his.

"We should move in here. With your family."

Dylan snaked his arm around Callista's waist, pressing his lips to her throat. "Really? Are you sure? And they are your family now too, yano?"

Callista turned in his arms, placing her hands on the sides of his neck. "You are happy here and I am happy when I'm with you. So, we should just stay here."

Dylan leaned down and kissed Callista softly on the lips, then held her close to him, her head resting on his shoulder as they waited with the rest of the family for news on mother and baby. In the distance, they heard the faint cry of a child, and the sound that had once filled them with a sense of dread, now felt like it had come full circle, an end to a turbulent beginning. It felt right, it felt sure.

So why the hell did Dylan have an uneasiness in the pit of his stomach?

CHAPTER TWENTY-TWO

Dante

Sharing a body and mind with a demon Prince was about as fun as it sounded.

Dante prowled at the edge of his body, caged by the demon he had welcomed with open arms. For centuries, Dante had been forced to sit back and watch as Vindicta searched for the damn pages of the book Dante should have left well alone. It was his own foolishness that had led them to this abrupt end.

It caused him some morbid satisfaction that his brothers and sister had managed to thwart Vindicta's plan to open a gateway to hell. It had made him laugh his ass off knowing that the cage his current roommate had built to hold the succubus, was now what kept him prisoner.

Dante stopped his pacing at the very moment he felt a new presence enter the basement-level cells. He had felt her before, this otherworldly presence that made him hunger for the first time in centuries. Vindicta became alert too…as if he too was entranced by the soldier who walked right up to the glass wall and stood, legs braced and arms folded across her chest.

The dragon was almost six foot, with chorded muscles and an air of no-nonsense. Her hair was cut short, it would have appeared masculine on anyone else but it made the angles of her face sharper, keener. Her cheekbones were pronounced, and her lips looked firm as she frowned, her eyes the colour of flames.

"How did you plan on obtaining a dragon scale for your spell?

You had the chance to take me and you left me on the ground bleeding?"

Dante felt Vindicta smile, felt his own anger bubble inside his consciousness.

"I had other options."

The dragon snorted, rolling her eyes. "I am the last dragon on earth. There are no other options."

Dante could feel the smug satisfaction ripple through Vindicta, as the demon Prince got to his feet, and walked to the edge of the bars. "Are you sure about that? Surely you have felt it, the pull, the tug calling to you. It's why you are here, right?"

The dragon frowned, shifting her weight. "Where are they?"

Fuck...so this was Vindicta's plot after all. And he had let himself be captured because he needed the dragon for some reason he had managed to keep from Dante.

"I will bring you to them. I will return to you the ability to change your shape and become a dragon once more." Vindicta told her, excitement in his veins, in Dante's veins but he himself felt sick to his stomach. "But you must do two little things for me."

And then Dante heard it, the tell-tale wail of a new-born child and his heart plummeted.

"I will not help you kidnap a babe."

Vindicta chuckled, running his hands over the bars. "First of all, I will need you to secure my release from this cage. I can't take you to your kin whilst confined in here."

Dante knew this wasn't the end and hopefully the beautiful dragon was not foolish enough to actually release them from the prison that kept Vindicta from hurting Dante's family. He could tell from the delight in Vindicta that the dragon had played right into his plan by coming down here to face him.

"And the last thing I will need from you is not to bring me the child. Oh no. I was wrong. The child's cries would signal the time was right to open the gate to hell. But the book, the book showed me exactly what I needed to become a god."

Dante tried to fight, tried to wrestle control of his body from

Vindicta to no avail and warn the dragon from siding with Vindicta, that no good would come of it.

But he could see that her mind was already made up, the chance to regain her dragon form too alluring, too seductive. And Vindicta knew that, not speaking again until the dragon did.

"Well, get on with it. What would you have me do?"

"It should be easy, dragon. Very easy for you." Then Vindicta laughed, making Dante shudder. "Leave the child with her mother. I have no use for them." The words of Lucifer's book that Vindicta had absorbed into his skin flared as the demon Prince smirked.

"Bring me the Obscurum alive and I will take you to your kin. Free me and bring me Ezekiel Collins. Then you will be whole once again."

This was bad...this was very, very, bad.

The Sicarius Security series
continues

FLAMES OF CONFLICT

SICARIUS SECURITY BOOK 5

SUSAN HARRIS

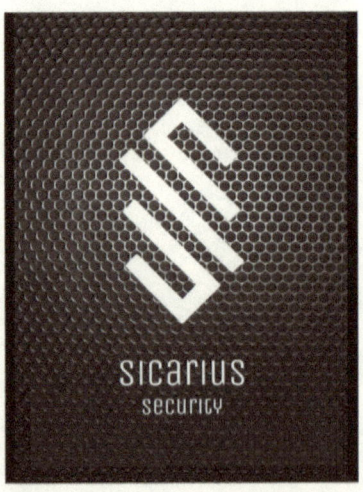

Coming August 2023

Dylan

1. Ruelle - War of Hearts
2. Palaye Royale - Dying In A Hot Tub
3. JC Stewart - Break My Heart
4. Twenty One Pilots - Tear in My Heart
5. Bring Me The Horizon - why you gotta kick me when i'm down?
6. Circa Waves - Fire That Burns (feat. PVRIS)
7. Nothing But Thieves - Honey Whiskey
8. PVRIS - Death of Me
9. PVRIS - Gimme a Minute
10. Rad Horror - Swallowing Emotions
11. KID BRUNSWICK - 4AM
12. Architects - when we were young
13. Too Close To Touch - Chasing Highs
14. Sigrid - Bad Life
15. Built By Titan - Times Are Changing (from the Freevee Original Series Bosch: Legacy)
16. Gaspar Sanz - Myriad
17. Alibi Music - Hunger
18. Palaye Royale - Broken
19. Zayde Wølf - Danger Zone
20. Sad Heroes - Sunny Side Down
21. Dan Lancaster - Phases
22. The Haunt - Why Are You So Cold?
23. KID BRUNSWICK - Bipolar Rhapsody
24. Too Close To Touch - Pick Me Up
25. All Time Low - Blinding Lights

26. Bring Me The Horizon - sTraNgeRs
27. Broken Hands - Wrong Track
28. Colin Stetson - Warm Shadow - Colin Stetson & Justin Vernon (of Bon Iver)
29. Architects - tear gas
30. Eminem - Is This Love ('09) (feat. 50 Cent)
31. KSI - Not Over Yet (feat. Tom Grennan)
32. VIOLET NIGHT - (if) you are the ocean (then) i would like to drown
33. MILKBLOOD - WICKED
34. MOTHICA - SENSITIVE
35. YONAKA - Anthem
36. VUKOVI - HADES
37. Goals - What Went Down
38. Akon - Smack That

Callista

1. ILLENIUM - Hearts on Fire
2. Movements - Colorblind
3. Twenty One Pilots - Not Today
4. Ganyos - Pressure
5. Bring Me The Horizon - mother tongue - Recorded at Spotify Studios NYC
6. 2WEI - Shape of My Heart
7. Tessa Violet - Games
8. The Maine - Black Butterflies and Déjà Vu
9. Death and All His Friends - Alone
10. TELLE - Crazy
11. guardin - alive
12. TELLE - Too Hard on Myself
13. Weathers - C'est la vie
14. Mother Mother - Hayloft II
15. Dream State - I Feel It Too
16. Fossil Youth - Nobody's Happy (feat. Kellin Quinn)
17. Mega - Box of Regrets
18. Jensen McRae - Wolves
19. Dia Frampton - Blind - Acoustic
20. Keir - Shiver
21. VUKOVI - SLO
22. PVRIS - Thank You (feat. RAYE)
23. Kintsuku - Enough
24. The Amazons - Ready For Something
25. PVRIS - Dead Weight
26. Two Feet - I Feel Like I'm Drowning
27. The Prodigy - Breathe (feat. RZA) [Liam H and Rene LaVice Re-Amp]
28. Grimes - We Appreciate Power
29. Fox Sinclair - Soft
30. Minotaur Jr. - Bad Moon Rising (feat. Alaska Reid & jonny gorgeous)

31. EQRIC - Dark Horse
32. deadmau5 - My Heart Has Teeth (feat. Skylar Grey) - From 'Resident Evil'
33. Tems - No Woman No Cry
34. Lizzo - About Damn Time
35. Nothing But Thieves - Unperson
36. Arctic Monkeys - Perhaps Vampires Is A Bit Strong But...
37. My Chemical Romance - Surrender the Night
38. New Years Day - Hurts Like Hell

ABOUT THE AUTHOR

Susan Harris is a writer from Cork, Ireland and when she's not torturing her readers with heart-wrenching plot twists or killer cliffhangers, she's probably getting some new book related ink, binging her latest TV or music obsession, or with her nose in a book.

Susan LOVES connecting with her fans!
www.susanharrisauthor.com